Price of Forbidden Love

by

Douglas Lowell Pemberton

DORRANCE PUBLISHING COMPANY, INC.
PITTSBURGH, PENNSYLVANIA 15222

ISBN # 0-8059-3788-9
Printed in the United States of America

First Printing

For information or to order additional books, please write:
Dorrance Publishing Co., Inc.
643 Smithfield Street
Pittsburgh, Pennsylvania 15222
U.S.A.

Dedication

*This novel is dedicated
to my daughter
Arista P. Pemberton.*

Contents

Introduction

Raggie was suffering from trauma, shock, and seizure-causing nightmares, from the devastating tragedy that would always haunt her total existence like the devil rising from his Satan-hellhole graveyard to take her back to hell as she remembered the night she came face-to-face once again with that one person she never knew existed, her father, George Rosemont, who had tried savagely to rape her. Her mind raced back from that day to the age of two, when Raggie first remembered her father slashing her mother Fannieo across her bare back with a bullwhip, striking her repeatedly, until blood flowed, for not having sex with him when he was drunk from corn whiskey.

Part I

"Price of Forbidden Love"

She was born in the year 1940 in Granada, in the midst of its rolling hills, valley, and farmlands with lakes full of catfish. The air was a pure quality not often found nowadays, except maybe sitting on an ocean cruiser in the middle of the ocean; there was no pollution of any kind, except maybe a tractor plowing the farmland of abundant crop production. Raggie's parents were farmers; her birth was to a farmer known for miles around in the little farm town of Granada, Mississippi. Raggie's father's name was Big George Rosemont and his loving wife was called Fannieo.

Big George Rosemont happened to have a drinking problem he acquired from the hard labor he put into the farming of his land. His wife, an Indian from the Chickasaw tribe, resented his drinking of alcohol because it brought on a hot temperament, which resulted in him occasionally beating her when he became totally drunk. However Big George was very popular because of his abundant crops he hauled into town every year at the end of the peak harvest season: corn, potatoes, greens, tomatoes, cabbage and fruit such as apples, peaches, cherries, plums, grapes and strawberries.

There was a farmer that lived across the dirt road who had eyes for his woman, Fannieo. His name was Felixo Blackmond, and he was also of the same tribe as Fannieo. He resented the beatings given to Fannieo by her husband, a white man, when he had too much alcohol to drink. At the age of two, Raggie's mother took her and ran across the dirt road for protection from the drunken son-of-a-bitch, for he had picked up a bullwhip to slash her across her back for not drinking with him. Felixo comforted and protected her and Raggie from the devilish, low-life, drunk, son-of-a-bitch, with his rifle pointed in Big George's face as he came chasing her with his bullwhip in his hand.

Felixo yelled, "Stop right there, or I'll blow your head off, and put down that goddamned bullwhip. You ain't got no right beating this woman like a piece of meat; if you don't want her, I'll keep her and marry her too."

Big George yelled, "All right, don't shoot." Dropping the bullwhip, he shouted, "OK, keep the goddamn cow-looking bitch and her ragged-ass daughter for that matter." From that day on, Felixo, Fannieo, and Raggie lived together, the adults getting married after Felixo paid for Fannieo's divorce attorney. When the divorce was final, Big George Rosemont married another woman who drank alcohol.

At the age of two, Raggie had a new father, after not really knowing her real father, who was a drunken bastard who would bullwhip her mother because she didn't drink alcohol with him. Raggie's stepfather was just the opposite of her father; he didn't drink or beat her mother, he was a very peaceful, understanding, gentle, kind, loving, sincere, church-going Christian man who feared no other man standing on the face of the earth.

The years passed swiftly, as they lived the simple life of farming the land and hauling in the crops, year after year. Then the sudden start of World War II frightened every human on the face of the planet, and the dropping of the atom bomb wiped out a complete civilization of people on an island. World War II escalated to heights of human destruction and total mayhem to the point where only God could save the human race from the total extinction of being erased from the planet Earth.

The war needed financial backing and the country of America was going financially broke, trying to stop the Germans and Japanese from taking over the whole planet. Gold was the main source of financial backing for this country to buy and supply itself and its allies with weapons, food, shelter and clothing. The America gold rush was on in Granada, Mississippi, and as luck would have it, Big George Rosemont had discovered gold on his farmland.

The mining of this precious gold went into mass production and Big George started getting very wealthy in the year 1945. The U. S. Government paid top dollar for gold found on Big George's farmland. A full year of mining caused the surrounding farmlands to become toxic because of the explosives used to help in mining the valuable gold. Since the U. S. Government was responsible for destroying the surrounding farmlands, it paid the farmers what the worth of the land was thought to be at this time of war.

Felixo's farmland was one of the lands that became toxic, poisoned because of the mining of the gold that used high explosives on Big George's farmland across the dirt road. So the government paid off Felixo Blackmond for the destruction of his farmland, as he was not able to grow one single crop of any kind. The high explosives used in mining the gold were too much for God's country, and Mother Earth ceased to replenish Felixo's farmland with the abundance of crops as it had done in the earlier blessed days of prosperity.

Now Raggie, five years of age, did not fully understand why there was a war and why humans killed each other, nor did she understand why Felixo had to sell his property to the government. Felixo accepted the government's payoff for the destruction of his land, and he and Fannieo and Raggie moved up north, to Chicago's south side, where it was just the opposite of where and what Raggie was accustomed to. Adapting to an entirely different environment was somewhat difficult, especially in a large city like Chicago. Felixo hated Big George more than ever for allowing the government to mine gold on his land, destroying all other farmland surrounding his property. Felixo, Fannieo nor Raggie ever realized that Big George Rosemont became a billionaire from the gold found on his property. Yes, Raggie's real father was a billionaire and she never knew it at her young age, nor did Felixo or Fannieo give a damn, as they could only think about their farmland that had been ruined by their greedy, drunken, woman-beating, son-of-a-bitch neighbor, Big George Rosemont.

The house Felixo bought from the government lump-sum payment for destroying his land was not much, because the government only gave him about $5,000.00. It was only enough to buy a two-bedroom house located on some sand dune full of ragweed, mosquitoes, fleas, flies, cockroaches, mites, and rats. The air was polluted from the steel mills, and garbage pollutants also burnt the nostrils of Raggie's nose, and her throat was clogged from all the ragweed pollen floating in the air. Raggie developed severe sinus problems as the days added up from her presence at her new home. She was stuck sitting in the middle of nothing but sand that could grow nothing but ragweed and bred nothing but mosquitoes, fleas, flies, cockroaches, mites, and rats. The government definitely put them in a hellhole, with gray skies from the steel mill pollutants with their smelly odors, a yard full of mosquitoes, fleas, flies, and ragweed, in a hot and humid summer—what else could you ask for in hell. Just the opposite from their heavenly farmland in Granada, Mississippi, every house looked the same as Raggie's home, all on the same sand dune full of ragweed and bothersome insects. To make matters worse, the garbage collectors came by every week to pick up the trash with rats and roaches jumping out of their truck that they had collected from the city garbage dump. Yes, the garbage collectors would come and pick up Raggie's trash, but left behind an occasional rat or cockroach to become an instant "pet" of Felixo, Fannieo, and Raggie's household hellhole. The sand dune dump the Blackmonds lived on couldn't grow any grass or trees either, and of course not any vegetable or fruit produce like Felixo's farmland.

Felixo Blackmond had lived off the farmland to feed and clothe his family in Mississippi, but he couldn't do the same in Chicago. So he and his family applied for county assistance and welfare like everybody else in their sand dune, a loud, smelly, shit-odor polluted neighborhood full of ragweed and insects that made their lives miserable. Their neighborhood plumbing caused the smell of shit, with plenty of toilet bowls malfunctioning so that there was shit to the very rim. An occasional shit flood would fill their streets made of asphalt and tar, making the whole neighborhood smell like shit, and people got stomach pains, yelling, "Where is the damn Pepto Bismal and Alka Seltzer?" on hot humid days in the heat of the summer.

The county handed Felixo and his family food stamps to shop for food and groceries at the only government-subsidized surplus food market, where the farmers like Felixo would throw away crops of vegetables and fruit product damaged from the insects or early morning frostbite, or sell them to the government at wholesale prices. To Felixo and his family, the food at the government food outlet was nothing more than something a farmer would have thrown away or garbage.

So there they were, taken from their paradise on earth to a sand dune ragweed trash dump to eat garbage like the rats from the local city dump. Felixo was depressed and ashamed of himself for settling for the $5,000.00 and for buying a house that they could barely breathe the air in. Even as the U. S. Government, known as Uncle Sam, won World War II, Felixo and his family lost everything, seeming like the enemy themselves. The only clothing they could afford or manage to get a hold of came from the Salvation Army or the local church helping the needy. The death rate was high because of the lack of medical attention needed to combat the diseases plaguing the neighborhood because of the living conditions they were forced to deal with. Every winter, a large number of poor people died from a simple cold or the flu.

The only self-help program the government offered Felixo was the trade school about a mile down the road across the railroad tracks, and you had to know how to read the English language, but Felixo couldn't read English at all. The main reason Felixo couldn't read English was because he never had to, not as a farmer; there was no need to read. How Felixo would meet the needs of his family was what he was the most ashamed of, because he knew he couldn't without his farmland as farming was all he knew, although he had free utilities, like electricity to turn on the lights to see his "house pets," the city dump rats and cockroaches, making themselves at home.

Felixo, seeing that the government was full of shit after almost dying from the winter's bitter, cold, sub-zero temperatures, decided to rob a city bank. This was the only way Felixo could provide for his family after the government had made a toxic wasteland out of his farmland, mining for gold to help win a war that put him and his family in a concentration camp. This, Felixo thought, was the only way to get even with the government, by taking back the money it had taken from across the dirt road with the gold mining that destroyed his farmland. So, seeing that he was right in what he was about to do, Felixo went to the gun shop to purchase a thirty-eight caliber revolver with the money left from the lump-sum payment the government thought was fair for destroying his land in a time of war. After he purchased the gun, he planned to rob the Chicago National Bank a week from Friday, when there was a big crowd of people at the bank during the rush hours between 3 P.M. and 5 P.M. in the afternoon.

Hating the thought of not being a man, unable to provide for his family, running to the government for help—the very government that put him and his family in their situation—was eating away at his heart and soul. Felixo was unlike the other men in his neighborhood, who turned into alcoholics or heroin addicts because of the same reasons—unable to be men and provide for their families. Instead they turned into beggars of the government who would issue them food stamps to buy garbage from the local government food outlet, or go and stand in a long line at the Salvation Army, waiting their turn for clothing handouts. The only way to be a man, Felixo thought, was by taking money from a bank, the same way the government took gold from the land across the dirt road from his farm. In Felixo's eyes, the government didn't want Felixo to show his manhood so that his wife and child could be proud of him. In Felixo's eyes, the government wanted him to be a beggar with no self-respect or self-pride, and to die at an early age from alcoholism or from a drug overdose, or maybe from the winter's bitter, sub-zero temperatures which Felixo and his family weren't accustomed to. Felixo's mind was set on robbing the Chicago National Bank of all the money in the bank, not missing a penny.

Friday morning came quicker than Felixo thought, as he waited eagerly for the rush hour to start so that he could become a man once again, providing for his family without begging from the government for food stamps, or standing in line at the Salvation Army waiting for clothing handouts. Felixo stood outside of the Chicago National Bank with his gun hidden inside his winter coat. It was cold outside in the month of February, but not sub-zero weather that day. It was almost 3:00 P.M. Only fifteen more minutes before the rush hour started. Felixo also had a brown suitcase in his right hand to put the money in. But he had no wheels or car to get away in after he robbed the bank. Felixo planned to take one of the bank customers hostage, using their car for the escape. Only two minutes before the rush hour and Felixo had a note on which he had someone write the words, "Give me the money." He was supposed to hand the note to the teller, open his brown suitcase, pull out his handgun on the tellers to make sure they put all the money in the brown suitcase, and finally grab one of the customers for a hostage, using his car to escape the security guard which Felixo only saw one of inside. Three P.M. on the button and Felixo ran inside with his suitcase, opening it on the counter in front of the tellers, taking out his note, and pulling out his gun. There was a loud bang, a gunshot from a plain clothes security guard, which went right into Felixo's head, killing him instantly.

Fannieo and Raggie received word of the sad news from a police officer who came from the Chicago police station to report this tragic incident to Felixo's family. Fannieo burst into tears and Felixo's body had been cremated, burned to ashes at the local county hospital. His ashes were given to Fannieo by the police officer in a little box the size of a matchbox. The police officer left with a smile on his face, as if to say well, that's all of that. Having to tell Raggie what happened to Felixo was very painful for Fannieo. Raggie, fifteen years of age at this time, teared in both her eyes, knowing Felixo existed no more. Felixo had died trying to be a man in a strange world he was not accustomed to, trying to provide for his loved family. Raggie never knew the truth about what really happened, because Fannieo told Raggie that Felixo died from the flu. Only about ten years in Chicago and Raggie had lost a loved one she never would forget.

Years swept by one by one, and Fannieo and Raggie also got fed up with the shit the government handed them on that sand dune that was covered with ragweed, full of insects, rats and cockroach infested, a shit-smelling hellhole. All the food stamp garbage bought at the government outlet garbage food chains gave them both diarrhea on a daily basis. So Fannieo and Raggie decided to become neighborhood hookers, like all the other single parent, hard-black bitches. Prostitution was a very profitable business, as long as the hooker stayed on her corner and nobody else's. Fannieo was about forty-two years old now, with Raggie at the ripe age of eighteen. Fannieo figured she had too many moles on her ass to turn any more johns or tricks, so she watched out for Raggie like a pimp would, while she was busting penis-ball nuts. Occasionally, Raggie would catch a sex disease from an uncleaned dickhead and go to the county hospital for butt shots the hookers called "VD shots."

One of the neighborhood pimps was interested in Raggie because of her shapely ass, attractive facial features, and her aquamarine blue eyes. The pimp, called Fast Eddie, wanted Raggie all to himself. He noticed how Raggie would stand on the corner and every twenty minutes have a new trick. Fast Eddie also happened to be a police officer, on the take of anything and everything. He sold the hookers heroin, or "mac," for their trick money also, and all the street hookers knew him as "Daddy Mac." Fast Eddie was looking for a new trick to be his main hooker or "hole" and he eyed the hell out of Raggie's shapely ass as she stood on the corner signaling for new tricks in her tight-fitting, above the knees, loud, red, lamb dress, showing her breast off in her low-cut see-through top that was bright yellow. Why Fannieo had Raggie tricking nobody knew, except that all the Chicago Public School Board had taught Raggie was the "Lord's Prayer," and "I Pledge to the American Flag," which was not enough to make a living off of and have the American dream and apple pie too.

Fast Eddie approached Raggie on foot one night as she was standing on her corner whistling at tricks driving by in their cars. He said, "Hey baby, what's your name, bitch, and what the fuck you doing standing on my hole's corner for, taking all her trick money?"

Raggie asked, "Who the fuck you talking to, punk?"

Fast Eddie replied, "You are my hole now, bitch," pulling out his police badge to show that he was a real punk cop.

Raggie said, "Oh, so I guess I'm under arrest and for what, son-of-a-bitch?"

Fast Eddie said, "For prostitution, a $50.00 fine or one day in the slammer."

Raggie pulled a fifty-dollar bill from inside her breast, and handed it to Fast Eddie, who took the money and said, "So you think you can buy your way out of this one, uh? Now you're really in deep trouble, bitch." He told Raggie to turn around so he could put on the hand cuffs. Raggie turned slowly around, shaking somewhat, showing she was nervous and suddenly broke into a run across the street, but Fast Eddie caught up with her, instantly tackling her on the concrete street.

Putting the handcuffs on her, he stated, "Now I really got your ass, on one count of prostitution, one count of trying to buy or bribe me from doing my job and on one count of resisting police arrest. That's a total of three counts. Bitch, you're looking at a year in the state pen." Raggie started crying, with tears rolling down the cheeks on her innocent-looking face. Fast Eddie walked Raggie to his pink Cadillac automobile, and put her in the back seat. Raggie teared more and more as Fast Eddie stared at her, looking as cold as ice.

Fast Eddie said in a smooth, calm voice, "Now look, bitch, I got your ass, and you can trick for me, or do a year in the state pen." Raggie, crying louder than ever, only eighteen years of age and having never ever seen or been in a jail cell block, shouted, "Ok! Ok! Ok!!! I'll do anything you say, just don't take me to jail." Fast

Eddie handed her a bag of cocaine, took the handcuffs off of her and said, "Take a hit."

Raggie said, "What do you mean? I don't use dope."

Fast Eddie struck her across the face with the back of his hand, saying, "Did you hear me, bitch, I said take a goddamned hit of that shit, before I hit you again."

Raggie, starting to shake, replied, "Ok, ok, ok!!! Mister policeman, how am I supposed to take a hit?"

Fast Eddie answered, "By putting a little fingernail tip of the shit up your nose, before I kick your ass." Raggie did exactly as Fast Eddie demanded, taking one hit after the other until her mouth popped open and Fast Eddie swiftly shoved his penis in her mouth. Fast Eddie said, "Suck, suck, suck my dick, bitch."

Fannieo was watching every second of what was going on, not realizing the man in the pink Cadillac with Raggie was a police officer. Fannieo ran to the pink Cadillac, yelling, "Oh, my God, stop it, before I call the police."

Fast Eddie looked at Fannieo as if surprised, saying, "Get the fuck out of here, you crazy, old, funky bitch, before I blow your fucking brains out." Fast Eddie pulled his forty-five caliber, semi-automatic hand pistol with a gold and pearl handle, and pointed it at Fannieo, trying to scare her away from what was happening as he was trying to make Raggie into his hole bitch. Raggie panicked, her eyes wide open, and pushed the barrel of the gun into Fast Eddie's head. There was a loud bang and Fast Eddie fell over into Raggie's lap, bleeding from the bullet that entered in his skull.

Fannieo shouted, "He shot himself." A large sum of money fell on Raggie's breast from Fast Eddie's shirt sleeve while she was pushing the dead pimp son-of-a-bitch pig off of her lap. She jumped out of the car, taking the money from Fast Eddie's dope pushing operations, and she and Fannieo ran off into the darkness of the night, hearing police sirens closing in.

The next day, Raggie and Fannieo couldn't believe their eyes, counting the dead pimp pig's dope money. There was almost $15,000.00 in hard cold cash, more than Raggie or Fannieo had ever seen before in their lifetime. Fannieo and Raggie decided to move to another side of town, since all the hookers on that street lived in the same neighborhood that they did and they were all suspects in the accidental death of a Chicago police officer. So, getting ready to move from their shit-bowl quarters sitting in a sand dune, full of ragweed and mosquitoes, and having the same standard of living as the rats and cockroaches they had for house pets, they gathered the $15,000.00 into an old black leather suitcase and caught a taxi to the other side of Chicago.

Months of looking for the killer of the local joketto-pimp-ass pig yielded no clues, as the taxpayer's money was spent to find his killer, which was none other than himself. So the Chicago Police Department finally closed Fast Eddie's case by writing him off as self-inflicted suicide. The oppressor of the unfortunate finally got what he deserved, death the same way he was giving death to the less fortunate poor, the poverty-stricken, sand dune, rat-infested and disease-plagued people the government handed shit after shit to by police heroin pushers, keeping them in a state of mind of hopelessness and depression, with no way of getting out of the hell they were in except by purchasing a cheap high that put them on cloud nine for a while—yes, heroin, nicknamed "mac," at five dollars a hit.

The hellhole Raggie escaped from, she never wanted to return to again—it had brought her memories of misery and hatred from the U. S. Government in disguise. The government was responsible for the situation Felixo, Fannieo and Raggie were put into—a sand dune of nothing, just waiting to get duned. Faith turned the wheels of fortune in the favor of hope, with the $15,000.00 from the people of the land of the dune in the hands of Fannieo and Raggie. Fannieo purchased a house much better than the one on the sand dune hell. Their new house had no ragweed growing in the front and back yard, breeding mosquitoes, fleas, and flies; there were no rats or cockroaches left by the garbage collectors, giving Raggie her awful sinus problems. There was no sand with the smell of shit and the steel mill's pollution burning the inside of Raggie's nostrils and throat.

On the other side of town, there was green grass in the front yard, no ragweed in any yard in the neighborhood. There were big beautiful trees, almost like living in a forest, except Fannieo and Raggie had a house built out of redwood with no mosquitoes, rats, mice or cockroaches for household pets. The sky was remarkably different; it was blue, reminding Raggie of her farmland back in Mississippi, and not gray skies full of steel mill pollution that burned the eyes, nostrils, and throats of everybody living on the sand dune hellhole. The air quality was fresh, and Raggie could actually breathe better, so her sinus problems went away.

The garbage collector's trucks were clean, not dirty like that on the dune side of town, with rats and cockroaches with well-known first names like Jimmy the Rat and Sally the Cockroach, jumping out and finding a new home every week. The streets had no rats named Jimmy and cockroaches named Sally, Fast Sally that is, running back and forth across the street, trying to decide which house had the best dinner plate. With $10,000.00 cash, Fannieo bought a house with no questions asked about where the money came from, no questions asked at all.

With the $5,000.00 left from Fast Eddie's dope money, she put Raggie in a professional school where she would learn more than, "I pledge to the American flag" and "The Lord's Prayer." Fannieo put Raggie in the school of pre-law, a two-year training career program to learn about the basics of law. Raggie's instructor was Mr. Freddico.

Mr. Freddico was not supposed to teach why the police sold welfare and county recipients hopeful dope, or why the government could fuck up her stepfather's farmland and put her in a sand dune dump, plagued by diseases not even discovered yet, like the one called "niggeraidoutist," with alcoholics and heroin addicts dropping like flies as though the insect spray "Raid" had come to town and knocked them dead, with rats and cockroaches taking over the shit-bowl house quarters because the garbage collectors dropped them off in your front door. One might wonder why Fannieo wanted to send Raggie to school after all she'd been through.

Mr. Freddico was supposed to teach Raggie why America was great, protected by God, stood for peace, liberty and justice for all, although this was probably a very difficult job for Freddico, after Raggie had been shit on all of her life in the big city of Chicago. Raggie's mother had her daughter prostituting, selling her body, just to make ends meet, after her body had played out due to moles on her ass, and after her beloved husband was killed trying gain back his manhood and start providing for his family again by robbing a Chicago city bank. To make Raggie believe America stood for "justice for all" would be a big accomplishment. Fannieo wanted Raggie to learn about American law with hopes of getting her dead husband's farmland back, seeing how hard life was in the big city of Chicago. Raggie, convinced that her mother was doing the right thing by sending her to pre-law school, decided to put her best foot forward. Freddico, like Fast Eddie, admired Raggie's shapely figure and innocent, sweet-looking face.

Meanwhile, Rosemont, back in Granada, Mississippi, richer, greedier, and bigger than ever, decided to move to Chicago with his alcoholic wife. Big Rosemont was a stone drunkard for sure by now, as his favorite pastime was sitting around his goddamned mansion getting drunk and urinating alcohol into his toilet bowl. He finally sold his damned mansion and moved to north Chicago's best neighborhood. He had no idea of his bastard daughter's presence there on Chicago's west side, attending pre-law school.

Raggie really did not remember too much about Big Rosemont after leaving his abusive ways full of alcohol at the early age of two years old. Raggie didn't remember her father's real name or remember what he looked like. Raggie didn't even have her real father's last name; she had the last name of her stepfather, Felixo Blackmond. Raggie's full name was Raggie Felixo Blackmond, and her mother had no birth certificate to show her otherwise. Fannieo never told Raggie her real father's name, so as not to bring back any bad memories of the past beatings from Big Rosemont. The north side of Chicago was where Big Rosemont bought his gorgeous marble mansion, on ten acres of land full of trees almost looking like a forest. The streets were super clean, with no litter of any kind. There was no crime rate to speak of, except for occasional domestic family violence. No police cars or corrupt police were in the area, like in the sand dune ghetto where Raggie became a hooker.

Here in North Chicago, every mansion pretty much had their own private security that patrolled the area on a frequent basis. Big Rosemont also forgot what Raggie looked like when she was just two years old, only remembering how much alcohol was left to drink. Big Rosemont's wife knew he had a daughter and she always had in mind to kill her if she ever showed up at their new mansion, for fear of her trying to take it over and maybe even Big Rosemont's first will. Only Big Rosemont's wife knew that Raggie had rights to her real father's will, and her real father was a billionaire. Big Rosemont's wife hired a private detective to find the whereabouts of Raggie and her mother, so that she could arrange for Raggie's funeral by accidental death, or even murder if necessary.

No one even knew that Raggie Felixo Blackmond's real birth name was Raggie Fannieo Rosemont, the name that was on her birth certificate given to her by her father, Mr. Rosemont. Raggie had no idea that this was her real name and the one on her birth certificate at the recorder's in Granada, Mississippi. Big Rosemont never told Fannieo because he was too drunk from alcohol to tell Fannieo after

Raggie's delivery, and Fannieo was too weak to talk. All he remembered was the name Raggie. So Raggie's full name was the one she went by now, Raggie Felixo Blackmond, was fictitious, a false name and she never knew it. But Big Rosemont's wife did know Raggie's real name when her detective found out the very next day, after making a phone call to the recorder in Granada, Mississippi.

Mrs. Rosemont was hysterical when the detective told her about Raggie and told the detective to find her whereabouts and that she would pay him handsomely. Very enthusiastic, the detective proceeded in his investigation as to the whereabouts of Big Rosemont's daughter, Raggie. His first move was to find the whereabouts of Raggie's Fannieo, knowing that Felixo told Big Rosemont that he was going to Chicago before he left. This was the only clue the detective had in getting the information from his employer, Mrs. Rosemont.

So Raggie was in pre-law school with intentions of learning enough about the law of the land that governs theAmerican people to rightfully regain her stepfather's farmland back for her mother and move back to the grounds of Granada, Mississippi, where everything was perfect. Everything was so simple—living off of the land, with no worries, no misery. The one thing Raggie didn't understand was why she was brought to Chicago to suffer in a hellhole full of disease from unhealthy sanitary conditions, poor plumbing, poor trash collection, a rats and roaches' paradise on earth, with the foulest stomach pain causing odor, sand for a lawn growing nothing but ragweed, with pollution burning the hell out of one's nasal passages, causing major sinus problems and several asthma attacks, a cloud of black smoke the government named pollution that definitely shortens one's life span; and to top all this off, the winters are cold as hell with a windchill factor out of this world.

Why in heaven's name did the government insist that Felixo move to Chicago with only the $5,000.00 they gave him for fucking up his farmland. Maybe they hoped eventually he would get fed up with the goddamned shit and commit suicide from an alcohol or heroin overdose, like all the other unfortunate, condemned, experimental government jackasses. But in Felixo's case, he decided to become a radical and rob a bank with a gun in his stupid hand so he could feel like a man once again, with the pride and respect of providing for his family without begging from the goddamned-pimp-ass government that suckered him into selling his land after seeing nothing would grow on it after the government's mining operations fucked it up. Although Raggie's mother finally told her the truth about what happened to her stepfather, how he was killed trying to feed them, Raggie felt she owed it to her mother to try and fulfill her wish of getting back their former paradise.

Freddico helped Raggie as much as possible with learning the law of the land; for example about paying taxes, such as federal, state, city, county, sales and property taxes. Freddico made his point about how the country of America is run and governed from every American paying taxes, even when a person buys a loaf of bread or gets a gallon of gas for his automobile. Freddico explained to Raggie that the government is a country run off of every American citizen's money known as taxes, used to run or operate government functions such as the courts, police, fire, and state and county assistance programs, such as social security, welfare and subsidized food chain markets. Freddico stated that our taxes help protect our country against foreign invasion with our military power, the army, navy, air force and marines. Our taxes provide learning institutions, called elementary and high schools and colleges, to educate its people and help advance our country to its highest potential of excellence and to prosperity. Those who don't think or govern themselves accordingly have the option of leaving the country or to be imprisoned for their wrongdoing in confinement of steel bars called jails, prisons, state penitentiary and federal penitentiary. All taxes paid by the American citizen protect them and their loved ones, families, and friends from wrongdoers, by paying for police, federal agents, the CIA, and other agencies that protect and serve the public.

The American citizen wanted all these values stated in writing in a document called the Constitution of the United States of America. These values were voted on by each American citizen and a majority of votes could enact a new law of the land. Mr. Freddico taught Raggie the basic American law, including the fines of the city of Chicago in which she resided. Mr. Freddico called fines punishment by payment of money for wrongdoings, which were voted on by the American public, such as traffic tickets and imprisonment fines voted on by each American citizen and the majority of votes would enact a new law of the land. For the more serious wrongdoings such as murder, long-term imprisonment or even death were voted on by the American public. The job market in America makes the law of the land a solid and stable government, for the job market pays its employees and the employees pay taxes on their wage earnings. If people in this country didn't work, we wouldn't have a government at all, but a vast wilderness of wild, ungoverned people doing as they wish.

Mr. Freddico explained all this to Raggie with the utmost enthusiasm, hoping she would grasp all that he was explaining to her. Raggie understood every word Mr. Freddico told her, but somehow she felt she wasn't a part of the American government. A boiling hatred for the American government raged in her entire body, as she remembered the painful, full of hurt and shame hellhole, the "ragweed sand dune," the government put her family in.

Raggie was wondering why Freddico was so hooked on the same damned government that killed her loving stepfather. She couldn't figure out why Freddico was so in love with America, after the hellhole she had experienced. Freddico never in his life had experienced the same world as Raggie indeed, for he lived on the north side of Chicago, where everything was lush, pleasant, and heavenly. Raggie never knew his world existed; she had never seen a mansion in her life, or north Chicago where Mr. Freddico lived.

Raggie spoke out in class one day. She said, "Mr. Freddico, may I ask you a personal question?"

"Why, yes, Raggie," replied Freddico.

"Mr. Freddico, why do you worship America the way you do?"

Mr. Freddico replied, "Because I love America, and I'll like to see you after class."

Raggie anxiously waited for class to come to an end to see why Mr. Freddico was so in love with America, a country Raggie thought was full of trickery. Finally, class came to an end, and Mr. Freddico called Raggie to his desk with a smile of sweet delight on his face, glowing like the sunshine from the abundant, powerful sun.

"Raggie," Freddico said, "I'm going to take you to dinner and treat you as a woman should be treated."

"Why? What do you have in mind?" replied Raggie.

"I'm going to show you personally why I love America and why you and I are the law of the land. So allow me to treat you this evening to the time of your life, such that you have never experienced before in your life."

"Ok, Mr. Freddico, I'll allow you to do that this evening," replied Raggie.

So off together they went, Raggie's mind in complete wonderland, for she knew not of Freddico's world. Freddico drove a Mercedes Benz 700 diesel with leather interior, stereo sound, a Motorola phone, and power seats and windows. Raggie never before in her life rode in such a fine luxury car, as Mr. Freddico turned the corner, heading for his home in north Chicago. Raggie noticed the change of scenery as the Benz drove down Lakeshore Boulevard, along the monstrous Lake Michigan. She never before saw such a beautiful lake and forestry in her life, as the air became crisp and fresh, and perfectly clear skies shone above, with no pollution at all. The streets were crystal clean, with no litter or trash of any kind, or rats and roaches racing back and forth, trying to decide which house had the best dinner plate, like the hellhole she came from, the ragweed sand dune. The homes looked like castles for kings and queens, with green, grassy lawns looking like field to grow corn in. Some of the trees on the lawns had fruit growing on them. Raggie thought she was dead and in heaven, for she had never seen such a beautiful world, where everything was perfect before her very eyes. Raggie thought she was in a coach driven by angels headed to heaven to see God Almighty.

Freddico pulled into his driveway, where there were two angels made of clay and marble, opening the gate made of silver, to his all white marble mansion. Raggie almost wet her panties as Mr. Freddico turned off the car engine, looked at Raggie, and said, "My child, this is where I live." Raggie thought she was looking at God Himself, the one that took her from Satan's hellhole sand dune full of alcoholics standing on the corner, heroin junkies knocking each other off for little or nothing, and police cars sounding their sirens, going to a murder scene in Satan's daughter's house at the ragweed sand dune hellhole. A smile came across Raggie's face as a tear rolled down her cheek. Her savior had finally rescued her from hell, she imagined.

"Now are you starting to see why I love America?" said Freddico.

Raggie replied, "Kind of."

They walked into Freddico's house, after the door was opened by the butler, and the maid asked Raggie if she could rest her baby blue sweater. Raggie simply smiled, motioning no thank you with a show of her finger swaying back and forth. Freddico slowly walked Raggie through his living room, where there was a painting hanging on the wall of none other than the first president of the United States of America, George Washington. Raggie stared at the painting of George Washington as if in amazement, like why in the hell does a black man have a white man hanging on his living room wall?

Raggie asked, "Why do you have that white man hanging on your wall?"

Freddico replied, "My dear, that white man happens to be George Washington, America's first president, the forefather of our country. The one that started our American democratic government. That's why our country is so great: every American gets to vote on who they want for president. He was the first pick by the American public."

Raggie had a deep hatred for white men because a white policeman killed her stepfather, as she found out later from a friend. This deep hate for whites she kept to herself. Freddico told his maid to prepare dinner for two, asking what Raggie wished to have for supper. Raggie stated she would love fried chicken, sweet potatoes, greens, and apple pie with lemonade ice drink. Freddico stated that surely her heart's desire was his demand. The maid prepared exactly what Raggie wished for, while Freddico ordered lobster tail with shrimp, asparagus, and a baked potato, with a tossed salad with ranch salad dressing, and the table bar brought to his side upon his demand sometime during the course of the meal, along with a dessert bar made of different pies and cakes.

Freddico was entertaining Raggie with his orchestra piano while waiting for dinner to be served, when his next-door neighbors finally arrived home. They were none other than Raggie's real father and his whore wife, the Rosemonts. Freddico didn't know his next door neighbor and didn't give a damn, as long as they attended to their own business. The Rosemonts had only lived there a short time, about six months. Strangely enough, Rosemont was drunk along with his drunkard wife, and had forgotten his damned door keys. The two drunks decided to ask their neighbor if they could use the phone to call a locksmith to open their house door, their neighbor, of course, being Mr. Freddico, whom they had never seen before in their entire lives. Their breath had the loud odor of alcohol, and they both barely made it to Freddico's door, almost tripping over each other's feet. Mr. Rosemont knocked on the glass window hard as he could, not seeing the doorbell, and trying to keep from urinating on himself once again. The butler answered the door, stating, "May I help you please?" in a state of complete shock as he looked at the drunken son-of-a-bitch.

Mr. Rosemont, with a very loud, odorous breath of alcohol and showing signs of being highly intoxicated, replied, "Yes, yes, yes, why, yes, you can, is the owner home?"

The butler stated, "Why, yes, sir, one minute please."

Almost slamming the door in Mr. Rosemont's face, the butler went to get Freddico while the Rosemonts anxiously awaited his return. Mr. Rosemont was trying with a great deal of difficulty to keep from wetting his pants. Mr. Freddico finally came with the butler and Raggie. Raggie did not realize for one instant that she was looking dead in the face of her real father, the man she never knew before in her life, the one that left her mother with another man to keep him from beating her because she wouldn't have a drink with him. Raggie did not remember any of this, nor remembered standing by her mother's side as Rosemont, with his drunken self, turned away from fear of getting shot by her stepfather. Now they were facing each other once again, but neither one realized who the other really was.

Raggie stared at the drunkard as if wondering, "Who the hell are you?"

George Rosemont was barely able to maintain his composure, and about to wet his pants, speedily asked Freddico if he could use his rest room, while his wife asked Freddico if she could use his telephone to call a locksmith, finally introducing herself as Mrs. Rosemont, his newly acquired neighbor.

Mr. Freddico stated loudly, "What an unexpected surprise. Allow me to show you to the phone. Come this way, please."

While Mr. Freddico and Mrs. Rosemont were in the other room calling a locksmith, Mr. Rosemont came back and asked viciously where his wife was. Raggie so resented his tone of voice and attitude, and loud, odorous breath, that she almost forgot where she was, and was about to call her daddy a goddamned-drunkard-honky.

But regaining her composure and becoming cool, she simply stated, "Using the telephone."

Mr. Rosemont started staring at Raggie as if he knew her and asked if they had ever been in each other's company before, implying that she knew what he was talking about, like maybe they had had sex one night as a one-night stand.

Raggie denied it loudly, almost shouting, "Of course not," at the top of her voice. "By the way, what's your name?"

He stated his full name, and went on to brag about his being a billionaire and his profitable gold mining business until Freddico and Mrs. Rosemont returned from using the telephone, after ordering a locksmith to Freddico's address.

"Well, well, well, here we all are. Well, well, how about staying for dinner?" Freddico asked.

Raggie suddenly said, "Take me home."

Freddico stated, "Oh, okay, as soon as the locksmith comes. You don't expect me to disappoint my newly met neighbors; they have to wait until the locksmith comes. They forgot their keys and left them in their house next door."

So, Freddico introduced himself to the Rosemonts and to Raggie, a student in his law class, and without undue satisfaction welcomed them to his neighborhood and stated he was very pleased to meet them, under the circumstances. The maid shouted out that dinner was prepared and Freddico showed his invited guest, Raggie, along with his uninvited but more than welcome guests to his elaborate dining quarters outside under the moonlight, which was enclosed in a glass-style patio in his backyard, set fully aglow by his sparkling crystal night lights. The maid served each guest their heart's desire, and very pleased were the three guests of Freddico.

Not to spoil the evening, but not able to keep it shut from the influence of liquor motivating his trend of thought, Mr. Rosemont opened his mouth: "I'm from Granada, Mississippi. As a matter of fact, I was born and raised in Granada and am very proud to be a native-born Mississippian." He went on to say that the was a farmer until the government discovered gold on his land, right before the war ended. "Yes, sir, I'm proud to be born an American."

Freddico said, "Well, allow me to add to that. I became a millionaire when I handled and won a malpractice suit for a pregnant woman that lost her baby by a famous doctor at a well-known hospital in north Chicago that had to file for bankruptcy just to pay me and my client, Mrs. Dollar, off. The doctor used the wrong medication on my client that caused her to have a miscarriage. Well, Mr. Rosemont, we both have something in common—we both are rich."

"Oh, yes, Mr. Rosemont, you and I were born in the same city and state," replied Raggie.

Mr. Rosemont almost vomited his dinner. "Why, you must be fooling me," replied Mr. Rosemont.

"Why, of course not, Mr. Rosemont, why do you think such a thing?" asked Raggie.

"Oh, because I never ran across anyone born in my city before, that's all," stated Mr. Rosemont. "This evening sure is a surprise."

"We all must say so to that statement," replied Freddico.

Raggie, at this point, went into a deep meditation as if spellbound, as if she had seen the devil once again, and Satan had come into her paradise to take her back to hell, as she looked at Mr. Rosemont. She started seeing why both Mr. Freddico and Mr. Rosemont worshipped the American government. They were both rich, living in heavenly paradise as kings of the gods, without a worry in the world, because they both had found their peace on earth, they were free at last, thank God Almighty, free at last. They didn't have to slave for no other but their own desires, or to satisfy a need within themselves. The government was made stronger from these two men's fortunes by the tax on their profits. This is what Raggie realized from the brief conversation they had just had. They rewarded the government and the government rewarded them back with the finest America had to offer in reality; housing, food, a residential area, automobiles, and of course, their careers—Freddico, a lawyer, and Mr. Rosemont, a gold miner. Raggie set in her mind to be as wealthy as these two gentlemen, as part of her mother's wish, even if Mr. Rosemont was on the alcoholic side.

Mrs. Rosemont suddenly, for no reason at all, bluntly shouted out at Raggie, "And how old are you, my dear?" But before Raggie could answer, the doorbell sounded and the butler announced that the locksmith had arrived for the Rosemonts.

"Oh, my dear, thank heavens. Let's go darling, before you fall to sleep; you know you have a heavy schedule tomorrow, with several appointments," replied Mrs. Rosemont.

"Oh, honey, you're absolutely right. Well, nice to have met you, Freddico and Raggie, hope we get a chance to meet again," said Mr. Rosemont.

Freddico replied, "But don't be in such a big rush; please stay and finish your dinner."

"Sorry, and thank you kindly for your generosity and kindness," said Mrs. Rosemont. Mrs. Rosemont, had noticed a strong similarity between her husband and Raggie; their eyes were the same color, aquamarine blue, a rare eye color, and their nose shapes were identical. This is why she was so silent at the dinner table and eager to leave, because of this strong similarity and the same birthplace, a fact which had startled her throughout the entire dinner. Raggie almost looked like her husband's daughter, the one she had secretly hired a private detective to find the whereabouts of, so she could plot Raggie's murder and inherit all of her husband's estate without the interference of her husband's bastard daughter contesting her husband's estate, willed to his beloved wife. The butler showed the Rosemonts to the door and stated he was glad to have met them and hoped they enjoyed their visit.

The Rosemonts replied, "Certainly did, and it was a pleasure to have met you."

Mr. Rosemont said, "Hope to see you again." Three steps later, Mrs. Rosemont asked Mr. Rosemont if he had seen Raggie before in his life.

He burst out in a real loud tone of voice, saying, "Hell no, and please don't ask me that question anymore. My God, do you think I play on you or something? I have never been to bed with that woman before in my life or seen her or heard of her name, as a matter of fact."

Mrs. Rosemont said, "Then why are you getting so upset over such an irrelevant, simple question like that for? You raised your voice like I asked you for a million dollars or a new fur coat or something."

Mr. Rosemont replied, "Sorry dear, I guess it was the liquor. I had too much to drink again."

Mrs. Rosemont answered, "You always have too much to drink, you goddamned drunkard, and how in the hell is your detoxification program from the damned shit you drink all the time going?"

Mr. Rosemont said, "Oh, honey, it's going great, they said I might not need artificial kidneys if I stop completely."

Mrs. Rosemont said, "Then why in the hell don't you; I'm tired of smelling your filthy breath all the fuckin' time."

Mr. Rosemont shouted back, "And damn it, I'm tired of hearing your rattling mouth shooting out profanity every other second,"...et cetera. Their normal heated conversation roared through the night, while the locksmith finally opened the door.

Mrs. Rosemont snapped, saying," When was the last time you saw your goddamned daughter; do you know what the fuck she looks like?"

Mr. Rosemont snapped back, saying, "Look, honey, I don't even know if she's living. I haven't seen her since she was two years old maybe, damn it, I don't even remember that or how her mother looked or my daughter's name. So please, don't ask me that question anymore." Mr. Rosemont paid the locksmith off and thanked him for his service.

Mrs. Rosemont said angrily, "Then why in the hell does that girl over there have your eyes and nose shape, dear?"

Mr. Rosemont, getting madder, his temper mounting, said, "Look, sweetheart, a lot of people favor each other. I saw this woman the other day that looked just like you."

Mrs. Rosemont, about to go off, said, "Is that right, sweetie pie?"

Mr. Rosemont, also about to go off, replied, "Yes, yes, sugar plum, and furthermore, I could give a fuck if she was living or dead, and let this be the end and final conversation about my daughter and past marriage."

Meanwhile, back at Mr. Freddico's estate, Freddico and Raggie were just finishing dinner. Freddico asked Raggie what she thought of his neighbors that he also happened to have just met.

Raggie instantly said, "Well, I think he's a goddamned drunkard who happened to strike it rich by being at the right place at the right time, and not all like yourself, who has something to offer the government besides what is laying around on your property. You have the right to be rewarded for your goodness, hard work, and making sure what's right is right and that wrong is wrong. I hope I can be a lawyer someday and help people who are taken advantage of to prosper and stride to the fullest of their potential, and not just let them waste away like an untouched, ripe, juicy, red delicious apple that has not served its purpose to strengthen the human race and wild animals that eat apples, like horses, and instead wastes away and becomes moldy and rotten and diseased like the people of the sand dune hellhole I came from. All the people in the neighborhood waste away, like in hell, with Satan keeping the gates closed for no exit. I think it's the shame of the nation to have its people waste away like they were meant to have nothing, to be nothing, and to do nothing but to drink alcohol, smoke cancer-causing cigarettes, make babies, fuck off day and night doing nothing but shooting dope in both arms until they become sore from needle points and drop dead from a sudden overdose like a cockroach sprayed with "Raid," the cockroach killer, or by the hand of another dope-ass junkie in need of a fix. I'm so happy to have moved from that hellhole; it almost seems like a miracle to leave the area and afford a little better standard of living, not living on the same level as the cockroaches named Fast Sally and the rats named Jimmy. I live where the garbage collectors don't leave as much garbage behind as they pick up, along with a new breed of cockroaches and rats. Yes, Freddico, you are a credit to our government and our race, you have achieved the highest standard of living America has to offer."

Freddico, astounded at what Raggie had just expressed, simply said, "Why, thank you very much, Raggie. I see you have learned quite a lot from your life experiences and of course, my law class, if you would allow me to say so."

Raggie responded quickly, "Yes, of course, I learned a lot from your law class and this delightful evening you invited me out on. To be frank with you, Freddico, I really hate to leave such an exquisite neighborhood as yours. I almost feel like a queen for day, with you of course being my king."

Freddico, waiting to hear exactly what Raggie had stated, replied, "Well, baby, let me tell you now, you can stay as long as your heart desires."

Raggie, surprised, said, "Oh, Mr. Freddico, I hate to take advantage of your kindness and warmth."

Freddico, getting eager by the minute, replied, "Don't mention it, baby, and please don't call me Mr. Freddico, just call me Fred, or baby."

Raggie, somewhat nervous at this point, exclaimed, "Why, Fred, you're making me blush and getting me kind of nervous. I have never had a man of your caliber come on to me like this before."

Freddico, making his move, announced, "That's because I want you for my woman."

Raggie, stunned, replied, "But we hardly know each other. I've only been in your class for only one semester."

Freddico, pressing the issue at hand, declared, "What does that have to do with it? When I first saw you, I had a strong desire to want to possess you, to own you, because of your glowing beauty. You stand out in my class like a pretty rose."

Raggie, blushing more, said, "Oh, Fred, I don't know what to say."

Freddico, pressing the issue harder, implored, "Please, please, please be my woman—I'll take care of you as if you were my wife," kissing Raggie on her cheeks.

Raggie, becoming somewhat nervous, said, "Baby, I'll have to think about it. With this type of question, I can't give you a direct answer right away. Please take me home now, you have gotten me all upset."

Freddico, somewhat upset also, but insistent, said, "Sorry to have done that; that was my least intention," kissing her again all over her blushing, rose-colored cheeks.

Raggie, finally giving in, responded with a kiss to Fred's lips. Their kissing lasted quite a while. Neither one said a word for a spell, after separating from each other's lips. Although Raggie really liked Fred, but didn't see how she could really love him, she plainly saw this as an opportunity to escape from the depressing, poverty-stricken area she was residing in that was one step from the sand dune hellhole she came from. She looked at Fred as the one who could take her from the world she didn't want to live in to the world of riches and prosperity, but most of all, freedom.

Freddico finally broke the silence, saying, "Will you be mine?"

Raggie, seeing a golden opportunity to escape hell totally, replied, "Why, of course, baby."

The kissing, accompanied with petting this time, continued into the midnight's fantasy. Raggie put into her mind that this was the opportune time. She wasn't going to let it slip by in the wind without putting her best foot forward, or should I say, her best showing. Finally, they were naked under the covers, having extreme, intimate sex, and arousing each other's curious natures as the night rolled into the morning dew with the break of sunlight shining into the bedroom. Raggie felt as though she was at home.

Suddenly she realized she had actually fallen in love with Fred. Neither one realized that it was morning or how fast time had slipped away as nature took its course in satisfying each other's human sugar fly.

Raggie suddenly realized her mother must be worried sick, and exclaimed, "Oh, my God, I have to call my mother to let her know I'm all right so she won't worry."

Fred responded swiftly to Raggie's demand, saying, "Okay, my sweetest." Calling the maid, he ordered breakfast and jumped into the shower while telling the maid to also prepare Raggie warm bath water. While waiting for her bath, Raggie called her mother and carried on a casual conversation about the lovely evening she had spent with her law instructor, saying how he makes her feel like she is somebody special and talking about his beautiful home and how they decided to go with each other almost like husband and wife. Her mother stated that she would love to meet her newly acclaimed love as soon as possible, if not this morning. Raggie assured her mother that everything was just fine and not to worry one bit, she was absolutely sure of seeing her this morning with Fred.

They arrived at Raggie's mother's house in a luxury car her mother had never seen before, or never even knew existed, and Fannieo was staring at it as it slowly coasted into her driveway. Raggie jumped out cheerfully, like a child with a new toy, and ran to her mother, kissing her on the cheek like never before, showing signs of being happy all over again, just like the time the pimp pig had left all the money on her lap when he accidentally shot himself in the head. Mrs. Fannieo Blackmond come outside to look at the fine luxury car. Raggie, happy, cheerfully said, "Here we are, just as I promised. Mother, meet my new friend, teacher and new lover, Mr. Freddico Jones." Her mother hesitantly shook Fred's hand, showing signs of being reluctant and not sure if he was the right man for her daughter to be with.

Freddico, with a smile on his face, said, "Well, pleased to meet you, Miss Blackmond. You have a fine daughter, a very bright student with a lovely personality, whom I can't stand to be without. She's my heavenly flower, sweetness all day and all night, like a fresh breath of spring. I can't breathe or function without her being by my side. She's the blood flowing through my body like the rivers flow through the earth to nourish and protect Mother Nature, as my Raggie nourishes my soul and protects me from getting ill by keeping me happy with her warmth, beauty, and radiant smile. Yes, Miss Blackmond, Raggie means so much to me, I would hate to lose such goodness that has brightened my life. She makes me feel younger, vibrant, full of energy, and ready to conquer the world. She's my queen and I'm her king. Miss Blackmond, she lights up my whole world, for without her my whole world would turn into complete darkness that has no end."

Miss Blackmond just simply said, "Well, if my daughter is happy, then I'm happy."

A big smile came over Freddico's entire face as Fannieo invited Freddico in their home, but he stated that he was in kind of a rush because his law class started in about thirty minutes. Trying not to be impolite, he had a seat next to Raggie on their living room sofa. Raggie went on to carry the rest of the conversation, stating that she had the same feeling for Freddico as Freddico had for her.

Raggie, very excited, went on to say, "And Mama, what a heavenly neighborhood Freddico lives in, you should see it. The homes look like castles for kings and queens."

Fannieo was on the edge of her seat, saying, "Really," with her eyes almost popping out of their eyeball sockets.

Raggie more eager, said, "Yes, Ma, and the lawns look like fields to grow corn in, they're so large with fruit trees. I have never seen so many fruit trees before in my life. The streets are so clean, with no trash cans or litter as far as the eye can see. Mother, the air is so fresh, I could breathe a lot easier over there."

Freddico, looking at his watch, exclaimed, "My, my, my, it's almost time for me to start to teach law. Nice to have met you, Miss Blackmond, hope to see you again." Kissing Raggie on the rosy cheek as he walked to his car, he told Raggie not to be late for his class tomorrow. Driving away, Freddico threw a kiss at Raggie and Raggie returned it.

Raggie went into a deep thought stretch, as though possessed by another person, off into another world. She was beginning to see how the government rewards its people for doing something or having something of extreme value, by only helping those that help themselves instead of wasting away in the wastelands of the sand dune ragweed hellhole, like Satan demands, drinking alcohol and shooting dope. She felt highly in love with Fred, knowing she didn't want to be without him or not in his world. Her determination to strive in the field of law as her mother wished was more a guarantee now instead of a promise. Freddico had definitely enlightened her on what she could obtain in the future. She was starting to realize that if one wants to waste away one's life, one can do so freely in the land of the free. One doesn't have to do anything, be anything, or have anything. A person can freely choose their own destiny; if they want to do something, have something, or be somebody, they surely can, using their heart, soul and brains. It is necessary to have the desire and ambition to obtain their goals in their life span, which is really such a short period of time, seventy to eighty years, when the planet earth has been here since eternity—millions and billions of years. One is here such a short time, it is such a shame to waste it away like who knows what.

The governing body of this country is made of and run by American people who have done the utmost for this country; they are dedicated, loyal, and patriotic with the same goal in mind—freedom for all to freely prosper in the avenue of life one chooses. America looks down on the ones that desire to waste away, letting them do so freely as long as they don't harm or bring down another that is trying to achieve the utmost of their ability in whatever field they happen to choose.

Realizing all this from her life experiences, she turned, after seeing Freddico's car disappear into the far distance, and walked inside to comfort her ailing mother, who was complaining of heart pain. Although Raggie was changing her viewpoint and opinion about America, mainly due to Freddico's guidance, she still had some doubts about the American system after being taken from her heavenly farmland in Mississippi to the hellhole sand dune. Why would America put her in a situation like that. She still felt cheated out of a good farm life, her heaven on earth, as well as her past stepfather.

Her mother also complained of breathing difficulties, due to the air pollution, and lack of good air quality her lungs were adjusted to as in Mississippi. Although their house had been paid for in cash with no questions asked, and Raggie's mother kept the deed to the house inside the sofa lining, there was the misfortune of not having enough money left over for hospital expenses after her mother paid for Raggie's entire law school tuition. The money was getting low from the pimp's dope money the Lord up above had blessed Raggie with that night. Every time Raggie took her mother to the hospital, the cost would steadily go up and worry would set in Raggie's mind as she wondered if her mother still had enough money to cover for this and the next visit, or enough if the hospital staff decided to keep her for observation, if they noticed some difficulty in the very near future. Although the Chicago County Hospital was free or could be paid by a small fee if the patient happened to have any money at all, the death rate at the County Hospital was three times as high as the hospital she was paying for, figuring it was well worth it. Her mother was still living, the only person she had left in the world besides her new love, Fred.

Raggie was still very excited and anxious to tell her mother more of what happened during her first evening out with Fred, and she said, "Mother, I met Fred's next door neighbors, because guess what, they locked themselves out of their house." At this point Raggie started laughing, while her mother started laughing with her, too. Raggie continued, saying, "His name is Mr. George Rosemont and he has the same color eyes as I do and also our noses are shaped the same, he has a gold cross, the one Jesus Christ was crucified on, on his front tooth, and Ma, Ma," Raggie was laughing even harder now, while her mother started getting silent, and her laughter totally ceased. Raggie started to continue, then noticed her mother's sudden change in appearance, haltingly said, "Rosemont said he was born in the same city as me and...Mother! Mother! Mother! What's the matter? Why are you acting like that?"

Fannieo was having flashbacks of her daughter's real father, and began gasping for air and holding her hand over her heart at the same time. Suddenly Fannieo fell to the floor, as if knocked down, choking for air, as it was getting more difficult for her to breathe. Raggie, nervous as hell, exclaimed, "Mother, Mother, Mother, please don't die." Raggie ran to the phone to call an ambulance once again, but it was too late. Her mother stopped breathing in Raggie's arms, as she was rocking back and forth, embracing her mother as tears rolled down her cheeks, crying and saying, "Please, God, don't let my mother die this time, please God Almighty, let her live one more day." Raggie started screaming, and getting hysterical, shouting, "Ma, please come back to life."

The paramedics arrived on the scene, and using breathing techniques and pulmonary resuscitation equipment that gave electrical shocks to the body, making her body shake, they tried to start her heart back ticking again. Time and time again, they tried with no success. Finally, the paramedics closed her mother's eyelids, covered her face and her entire body with a white sheet, and placed her body in a body bag to take to the county mortuary to be cremated. Raggie finally fainted and was immediately given oxygen and sedatives to calm her nerves, as the paramedic said to her in a soft voice, "I'm sorry, we tried the best we could."

Raggie stood in complete silence, crying, and watching them drive her mother away to be cremated in a gas incinerator, her entire body turned into ashes, to finally be given to Raggie to be stored away for memories' sake, knowing she couldn't afford a funeral, only the rich could. Raggie cried herself to sleep. The telephone started ringing off the hook the next morning, and Raggie was awakened by the constant ringing of the phone. In a deep state of depression, she did not answer the phone, and weeping still, she fell back to sleep, and ended up sleeping for days and eating nothing, finally making herself sick.

Bang, bang, bang—the sheriff's department was banging on the door, waiting for Raggie to answer. Finally, she opened the door, with her eyes bloodshot from not eating, depressed and stressed from her mother's death. She just stared at the sheriff's deputy, saying nothing. The sheriff, straight-forward looking, said, "Sorry, miss, but here are your mother's ashes from the cremation. Please sign your name here on the dotted line." Raggie nervously signed her name and took the box of ashes from the sheriff's deputy, saying, "Thank you very much." She again burst into tears, closing the door behind her and placing the box of ashes of her mother's remains next to her stepfather's box of ashes on the clothes dresser in her mother's bedroom. That was all Raggie had left in the whole wide world, two boxes of ashes of her only loved ones.

She fell back into the deep sleep that might eventually take her life if she didn't get something to eat, because signs of starvation were setting in. After not eating for almost a whole week, she had become not only sick but dehydrated as well from not drinking water, and skinny, losing about seventy pounds. Trying to sleep herself to death after losing the one she loved the most, Raggie was almost joined with her mother, about to die, but there were loud bangs at the door once again.

"Raggie, Raggie! Raggie!! Raggie!!!!" shouted Freddico, standing outside banging on the door. Fred had become hysterical, after not seeing or hearing from Raggie in over a week, and started shouting some more, "Raggie, open the door, it's me, Fred." He was screaming at the top of his voice, and about to kick the door in if Raggie didn't answer in the next several moments. Fred panicked, kicked the door open, and ran from room to room shouting, "Raggie, where are you?" Finally coming to Raggie's resting place, Fred froze in place, looking at Raggie, who had become very skinny and pale. Fred bent down over Raggie, softly kissing her on her cheek, which wasn't rosy anymore, and saying softly, "My poor darling baby, what the hell are you doing to yourself?"

Raggie, awakened by Fred's voice, just stared at him, incoherent, very weak at this time because of lack of food and water, and just a fragile little body. Finally a smile slowly came across her face, as she realized it was Fred, her one and only love. A teardrop crept down Fred's face as he smiled, seeing his love was still breathing.

Fred softly said, "Don't worry, baby, I swear to God I'll take care of you forever and ever until death parts me of you." Fred called the ambulance and Raggie was rushed to the hospital and placed in the intensive care unit because of starvation and dehydration.

As the years passed by, Fred and Raggie were finally married. They became Mr. Fred and Mrs. Raggie Jones, living happily ever after like in a scene in "Alice in Wonderland." Raggie finally became a lawyer like her loving husband, her dearest Fred. She had fulfilled her mother's wish like she guaranteed, and had become a worthwhile American citizen like her honorable husband, Fred. Fred had given her a new start in life, bringing paradise to her feet, having a rewarding law career with a castle to go along with it, fit for the queen she turned out to be. What more could her king Fred want, or Raggie for that matter? Yes, an American dream was fulfilled as written in the Constitution of the United States of America, freedom for all, and freedom Raggie surely had found. Mr. and Mrs. Rosemont, their neighbors, became close friends of the Joneses. Fred and Raggie Jones even took on a couple of lawsuits brought against Mr. Rosemont's gold mining business. They won the cases and were rewarded handsomely by Mr. Rosemont, Raggie Jones' real father, and did not even suspect him to be her blood father the least bit, nor did Mr. Rosemont, for that matter. Mr. Rosemont grew a special passionate feeling for Raggie inside of him, having thoughts of how it would be to make love and have sex to its fullest limit with the one he admired the most. Every time he saw her, that sensation would run through his body, and he would have to control himself every time he and his wife were invited to dinner at the Jones' mansion, assuring his wife he was not the least bit interested or attracted to Mrs. Fred Jones in any way or fashion, remembering how his wife had raised hell about their first introduction when they locked the keys in their house.

Mr. Rosemont and his wife really weren't on speaking terms though they seemed happy in public. In their house it was an entirely different story. They didn't sleep in the same bed or room, eat at the same table, use the same toilet bowl, or even look at the same television set together. They were barely around each other at all, having different schedules just to keep out of each other's sight, and most of all, to keep from getting on each other's nerves. It was entirely two different worlds under the same roof, and only the same roof because of a marriage license permitting such a relationship to exist. On occasions, they would ask each other where the other was going and what time one might be back, so as to make arrangements not to be there upon their return. This was especially true for Mrs. Rosemont; because of Mr. Rosemont's alcoholism, she couldn't stand to be around him, with his loud, very, very, very unbearable breath, uncomfortable and unpleasant to be around. Sometimes he would throw up or vomit on his clothes, making the entire house smell very, very, very obnoxious. This unpleasantness in being around each other in their relationship brought Mr. Rosemont's determination to a boiling point to have the opportunity of having sex with Raggie.

Raggie, much younger than Mr. Rosemont's wife, and a lot better looking with her natural beauty, used hardly any makeup, unlike his wife, who almost looked like a dead person, just having the finishing touches added to her face in a funeral parlor instead of a beauty parlor. Mr. Rosemont's wife also had excess weight in all the wrong places, like a double neck, a hanging stomach and a lumpy ass. His strong desire to have sex with Raggie no matter what, at any price was about to surface. Admiration of Raggie's slim and shapely figure was driving Mr. Rosemont crazy. He found excuses to visit the Jones' as much as possible, the usual excuse being the gold mining company's lawsuits.

The Joneses had the ideal marriage, and were both lawyers, working from the same office. Mr. Jones taught some night law courses, though. Both were making the U. S. government law work for them, and ensuring their clients, whomever they happened to be, that they got the best law that the U. S. American law and judiciary system had to offer. The Joneses did practically everything together: dining out, taking in occasional entertainment, and vacation tours overseas, like sightseeing in Europe, South America, and the Caribbean Islands. They slept in the same bed and were hardly never apart, except when Fred taught night law courses. This was the perfect opportunity Mr. Rosemont planned for to be finally alone with Raggie.

Meanwhile Mrs. Rosemont gave up completely trying to find out the whereabouts of her husband's first wife and daughter. After paying a private detective royally, who simply came up with nothing at all, no clues or traces of either's whereabouts, she became satisfied that they were probably already dead like her husband suggested upon their first introduction to Fred and Raggie. Mr. Rosemont's first wife, Fannieo, Raggie's mother, was dead from a heart attack aggravated from Raggie telling her mother about her first date with Fred, and meeting Rosemont, her father, at Fred's mansion. Raggie had described Rosemont perfectly by the gold cross on his front tooth, and the same color eyes that Raggie had, aquamarine blue. Also, he had the same nose shape as Raggie, but the gold cross on Rosemont's front tooth was the distinctive characteristic Rosemont had since he was married to Raggie's mother.

As soon as Raggie mentioned the gold cross on Rosemont's tooth, Fannieo knew the devil had risen again, and she remembered how he used to get stone drunk and beat her because she wouldn't drink with him. The aquamarine blue eye color of Rosemont and Raggie was also a rare eye color. Fannieo was assured that this was the same devil when Raggie mentioned her eyes were the same as his, causing the fatal heart attack in Raggie's mother from the awful memories she experienced with the devilish Rosemont.

So Rosemont, noticing Raggie was alone one night when Fred was teaching law and Rosemont's wife had a club meeting called "Millionaire Wives of America," thought of the perfect reason to go and see Raggie, who was sitting all alone in her castle, and try to have some of that long-awaited sex he had been longing for all these years, at any price.

He rang the bell of the Jones' residence and Raggie answered the door. Rosemont was surprised it wasn't the maid or butler, who both had the night off. Mrs. Jones said, "Well, how do you do, Mr. Rosemont, what a pleasant surprise. What brings you around this time of night? Did you lock yourself out again?"

Laughing to bring back memories of their first introduction, Mr. Rosemont replied, "Oh, no, I simply wanted to know if your husband was home so that he could help me with this law case that is pending tomorrow morning, before I go to court."

Mrs. Jones said, "So is it very important? Maybe I can help you with it; my husband is at law school teaching night courses and won't be back until very late."

Mr. Rosemont replied, "Why, of course you can, Mrs. Jones, you are just as qualified a corporate lawyer as your husband. Your husband has told me a lot about your advisement in more difficult cases. He even told me that without your expertise how lost he would have been."

Mrs. Jones said, "Oh, Mr. Rosemont, you're making me blush, but come on in and let me see what I can do to help you. Come right this way; follow me to my study so we can get right to the matter of business at hand."

Mr. Rosemont, certainly eager, said, "I'm pleased that you have decided to help me with this urgent law matter. I'm more than grateful that you have shown your interest in my problems."

Mrs. Jones said, "Oh, think nothing of it, Mr. Rosemont. It's my job to see that the law of the land is soundly and swornfully practiced."

Entering the study room, Raggie had Mr. Rosemont seated comfortably, and looked professionally at the lawsuit he handed Raggie, supposedly to be contested in court the next day. "Why, Mr. Rosemont," stated Raggie, "this case has already been settled."

Mr. Rosemont replied, "I know," staring hard and looking desperately at Raggie as if wanting something from her.

Mrs. Jones said, "But I don't understand."

Mr. Rosemont shouted, "You're my case," and ran over to grab Raggie around her body to show his wholehearted warmth boiling inside his body for her affectionate love.

Mr. Rosemont became hysterical saying, "Please! Please!! Please!!! God Almighty, please let me make love to you, to show you how much I care about you. I will buy you anything you want, whatever the price, your love is priceless to me. I can't sleep nights without thinking about making love to you. You're all I think about, day and night. My wife gives me nightmares."

Raggie, in a complete state of shock, was unable to say a word because of the sudden embrace by Rosemont, almost taking the wind out of her. She panicked, shaking, trembling, and nervous with sweat pouring from her forehead.

Rosemont started kissing her on her mouth, tearing her dress off completely, and wrestling her to the ground, about to snatch her panties off. But Raggie, regaining her wind, shouted, "Stop, you goddamned fool, before I call the police and have you locked up for rape. Did you hear me, damn it, stop! Stop!! Stop it, you're tearing my panties, goddamn it."

Mr. Rosemont savagely exclaimed, "Oh, baby, give it to me, come on baby, give it up, you know you want it as much as I do."

Raggie started screaming, "Help! Help!! Help!!! Somebody help me."

Rosemont put his hand over Raggie's mouth to keep her silent, while he maneuvered his body into position to sexually assault Raggie with his overpowering strength. Raggie started to bite Rosemont on his hand, the one covering her mouth, and on his neck, finally escaping the hold Rosemont had on her, and running desperately to her desk drawer to open it before Rosemont savagely grabbed her from behind. She pulled out a thirty-eight caliber hand gun, and turning and facing Rosemont, said, "Stop, you goddamned bastard, before I kill your damn ass!"

But Rosemont started laughing, saying, "You won't shoot me, bitch!" Rosemont took one step and Raggie shot Rosemont twice in the forehead and once in the stomach. Tumbling to the ground, Rosemont fell dead upon Raggie's feet. Raggie shouted, "Oh, my God, please forgive me!" Crying, tears running down her face, and trembling, she moved her feet from underneath the dead skull of Rosemont's bloody face. Shaking nervously, she walked to the telephone to call the police department. Raggie said, "I just killed a man trying to rape me in my house," as she was crying, at the same time telling the police department what just happened.

The police department stated, "We will send somebody over right away." Within minutes, a couple of police squad cars were out front of Raggie's house with their red lights flashing. Raggie nervously answered the door with her dress torn to pieces and her hair all disarranged, showing signs of a struggle, with Rosemont's blood on her feet. Rosemont was dead as a doornail, lying in his river of blood, as the two detectives felt for vital signs to see any signs of life, but there were none—Rosemont was dead as hell. Raggie sobered, looking down at a man who wouldn't stop trying to rape her, no matter how hard she pleaded. The detectives finally covering his body with a blanket, walked over to Raggie, saying, "Ma'am, he's dead." Raggie knew that this time was no accident, remembering the pimp-cop dope pusher who actually did shoot himself in the head accidentally. This time, she meant to kill this hellish mad man sent from hell by Satan to shame her womanhood. Raggie shot in self-defense this time for sure.

The detectives asked Raggie what had happened that resulted in a billionaire, the owner of a gold mining business, ending up dead on Raggie's study room floor. Raggie, emotionally upset and crying half the time, finally told the detectives why she shot Rosemont, as if they were blind and couldn't see her dress torn to pieces and her hair all a complete mess. It was hard to believe they didn't believe her, as if to say she staged the entire scene and were wondering what the hell would a billionaire want with a woman like this.

The detective stated, "There will be an investigation of what happened tonight, Mrs. Jones, because it's my job—not that I don't believe you." The detective's name was Mr. Peppervitch, and he finally gave his card to Raggie with his name, phone number, and which police district he worked out of. Two paramedics put Mr. Rosemont's dead body in a body bag and the detective stated he would keep in touch if something further developed. Raggie thanked the detective for his understanding and cooperation as she closed the door, running to call her husband.

Fred immediately drove home, almost having several accidents before arriving home. Fred was amazed at what he saw—Raggie looked like a Raggedly Ann doll with blood all on its feet. Raggie's dress was torn to pieces and Rosemont's blood was still all on her feet. Raggie was still too hysterical to take off the torn clothes and wipe off Rosemont's blood from her feet. Fred asked Raggie what happened, as she was comforted by his loving arms holding her tightly next to his strong body, saying, "Baby, don't worry, everything's going to be all right. Baby, don't worry, please, I'm here to take care of you forever."

Raggie was crying steadily as Fred called their private doctor to come immediately to their house. The doctor gave Raggie some sedatives to calm her nerves so that she wouldn't have a nervous breakdown and had his nurse tend to her bath, cleansing the awful blood from Raggie's feet. The sedatives put Raggie into a deep, placid sleep soon after the nurse helped her bathe. Raggie did not realize she had killed her blood father, the one she never knew after her mother remarried when she was just two years old, not remembering one thing about his facial looks or body appearance at such a young age. She never knew Rosemont used to get drunk and attack her mother, the same way he attacked her before she shot him three times to death, trying to keep from getting raped by a hellish drunken mad man who thought he could have anything and anyone he so desired, by of course putting a price on humans, like buying an object from a store.

But in Raggie's case, she was already wealthy and a prominent lawyer with high respect from her peers, neighbors, and city. Rosemont couldn't buy her like the rest of his human objects he manipulated like toys, although Raggie had past experience of being bought when she was prostituting because of need of money, seeing it as the only means of getting money in the sand dune hellhole she came from and having no education to get a job of any kind. She hated how she was selling her body, a sin and disgrace having strangers, mostly alcoholics and dope junkies, take advantage of her young, pretty body, with her mother assuring no harm would come her way. Rosemont's rape attack only made Raggie's rage of hate come to a boiling point, causing her to shoot her daddy dead.

Raggie, in a heavy sleep from the sedatives that weren't quite strong enough, woke up screaming and kicking, thinking Rosemont was still attacking her, ripping off her dress and panties and finally having his blood pour onto her feet. She thought she was walking in the blood of her father, a satan rising from hell to take her back through a hell she already knew.

Fred, not believing what he is seeing, says, "Baby! Baby!! Baby, it's me, it's me, Fred." Holding Raggie tightly in his arms to calm her nerves and keep her from shaking and trembling once again, Fred assured Raggie she was safe, saying, "Baby, it's going to be all right, I'm here with you, like always." He rocked Raggie to sleep like a newborn baby to keep her from crying.

Two weeks later, Raggie was almost over the terrible tragic incident, when a ring of the doorbell came at the Jones' door. The butler answered the door, saying, "Yes, sir, may I help you, detective?"

The detective answered, "Yes, I'm Detective Peppervitch, with an arrest warrant for Mrs. Jones for first degree contemplated murder."

Butler became hysterical, saying, "Oh, my God, dear heavens, I'll go tell Mr. Jones. One moment, please." Horrified, the butler panicked, and told Mr. Jones there was a detective at the door, saying nothing else.

Mr. Jones, finally facing the detective, asked, "May I help you please, officer?"

The detective said, "Yes, sir, Mr. Jones, your wife is under arrest for the murder of her father, Mr. Rosemont."

Mr. Jones, about to go insane, blurted, "Are you out of your fucking mind? Why, I'll sue you for stress, false arrest and goddamn it!...I'll...!"

The detective flashed the arrest warrant in Mr. Jones' face, assuring him it was the real McCoy. Mr. Jones, still insanely puzzled, shouted, "What the hell you mean, killed her daddy? Mr. Rosemont, he ain't her goddamned daddy, you crazy son-of-a-bitch, get the fuck away from my house before I call the real police department, goddamn it!!!" Mr. Jones, calming down his voice some, continued, "Mr. Rosemont was my client and not my wife's father, you smart son-of-a-bitch. She never ever knew her birth father, just her stepfather. Why in the hell are you playing with my mind like this? Are you drunk or something?"

The detective, getting angry, said, "Where is your wife, Mr. Jones? I know you're highly upset, but if you don't tell me, I'll lock you up also, damn it!"

Mr. Jones, getting angry, said, "Are you threatening me?" and balling his fist up, was about to strike the detective, but Raggie shouted, "Who is it, honey?"

Raggie was booked and charged with first degree contemplated murder, for the murder of her blood father, the motive being to inherit the billion dollar estate, the gold mining company and his real estate property. Her bail was $500,000.00, that her beloved husband, Mr. Jones, put up before Raggie went into a complete coma from the state of shock.

The district attorney, Mr. Diehard, and the detective, Mr. Peppervitch, wanted the electric chair and no less than life in prison from the superior court judge, and scheduled the case for the next month. Judge Barlor was known for giving the maximum sentences in cases like these. The district attorney had strong evidence against Raggie, the main piece of evidence being Rosemont's will, that read: "All my assets to be solely inherited by my only living daughter, Raggie Rosemont." Not even Rosemont's wife would receive a penny of his estate and assets.

Rosemont's wife was in the hospital, seeing psychiatrist for manic depression after the burial of her husband, and discovering she was not to receive a penny of his estate, she called her lawyer, trying to contest the will left for Rosemont's daughter. If she didn't and Raggie was found guilty or put to death, the State of Illinois would receive Rosemont's estate, and Mrs. Rosemont, not one single penny of it. Her attorney advised her she had the right to contest such a will, since she was his wife. Raggie, on the other hand, in total amazement of all that had happened so suddenly and tragically, still didn't believe all this was going on, and thought she was still in a deep sleep with all the sedatives her doctor had prescribed for her. In a world of tranquillity, an unreal world, a state of not existing, she placed her mind in a safe deposit box, not accepting anything that had happened and nothing that was said.

Weeks passed and the court date was nearing. Raggie was feeling sorry for herself because she had killed a man she barely knew, a client of her husband's, and most of all, her real father. She began to realize why her mother divorced the drunken, raping, son-of-a-bitch. Living with Satan, a mad man from hell, making her life a complete hell must have been awful, Raggie thought, realizing why her mother had a stroke when she described his looks—the eyes looking like hers, aquamarine blue; the nose shape the same; and the devil having a cross, made of gold, imprinted on his front tooth. The memories of his torture and physical abuse to her gave the last and final blow to her heart, causing her death.

Raggie's sudden realization that she had also revenged her mother's death caused her to stop feeling sorry for herself, and taking complete control of her emotions, nerves and state of mind, she took her mind out of the safe deposit box. She was determined once again to guarantee the wishes of her mother and herself and to clear her name of murder, to prove that the death of Rosemont was from the result of self-defense to keep from being raped, which is the right of every American citizen—woman, man and child. This thought, for self-defense, gave Raggie the peace within herself to fight for her freedom rights and to be proven by the law of the land in the American court system by a twelve-member jury. Only the jury would judge the guilt or innocence of Raggie.

Fred, astounded also that such happenings could occur in his lifetime, was behind his loving wife 100 percent. Although Raggie was an attorney, she can't defend herself or be her own attorney in a murder case against her, so Fred automatically became her lawyer. Fred was 100 percent confident that this would be a quick and short hearing, since the only evidence the district attorney had was the will of Rosemont, dated 1940, when Raggie was born. Fred investigated Rosemont's financial progress, recognizing that he became a millionaire after he was divorced from Raggie's mother and Raggie had no knowledge of Rosemont's will at hand. Never knowing who her real father was, she had moved to Chicago before he discovered gold.

On the other hand, the district attorney was to try to prove that Raggie did have knowledge of Rosemont's will and that she knew all along that Rosemont was her father and had planned the murder of her father to inherit the fortune by staging a rape scene and shooting her father. The day of court, Mr. Jones was confident of a dismissal, due to a lack of evidence and the case being solely based on speculation from Detective Peppervitch. The district attorney on the other hand, expected the death penalty, having had numerous cases of family greed amongst wealthy relatives. Judge Barlor called the court to order and insisted the jury of twelve members use their utmost judgment during and after the hearing, listening to both sides before arriving at their verdict, and weighing all the evidence. The main piece of evidence, of course, was Rosemont's will, presented to the jury by being read aloud by the district attorney. Mr. Diehard stated, "The will reads as such or as follows, stating that, 'My beloved daughter, Raggie Rosemont, would inherit all that is my wealth.'" That was all there was to the will, one sentence not in any way detailing the wealth, which Mr. Jones objected to.

"Your Honorable Judge, the will says, 'My wealth'. At the time the will was written, Rosemont had no wealth at all, or to mention, except his farmland, and no gold or minerals were discovered on Rosemont's land in 1940 when he made the will out. Matter of fact, according to his mining company's records, gold was discovered in 1950 on his farmland, after my client and her mother were already in Chicago, after moving out of Granada, Mississippi in 1945 or thereabouts, when the government paid her stepfather $5,000.00 for damages to his land. Government officials accidentally put dynamite on his land and when it exploded, they were hoping to discover gold on his land without my client's stepfather's permission, thereby ruining his crops and harvest for that entire year."

Judge Barlor permitted the objection and the district attorney Diehard rested his case, calling Mrs. Rosemont as his next witness. Mrs. Rosemont, fully recovered from the state of manic depression she was in upon her husband's sudden death, was hoping wholeheartedly to regain possession of her husband's estate, including the mansion and the gold mining company. Mrs. Rosemont happily took the witness stand, and gave the oath to tell the truth and nothing but the truth.

The district attorney, Mr. Diehard, asked, "Mrs. Rosemont, were you happily married to Mr. Rosemont?"

Mrs. Rosemont replied, "No, I wasn't, because of his alcoholism and his abusive behavior."

Mr. Diehard then asked, "Are you saying that you and your husband didn't get along?"

Mrs. Rosemont simply replied, "Yes, I am, that's why he always ran to other women, and furthermore, I don't see why Mrs. Jones is being accused of first degree murder because of wanting to inherit my husband's estate and assets. Mr. Jones, my husband's attorney, had my husband's will signed over to me a week before today because his wife, Mrs. Jones, refused to accept the will of a man she never knew was her real father, her blood father, who tried to rape her and take her pride and dignity."

The judge shouted, "Case dismissed, due to no grounds or substantially sound evidence. Mr. Diehard, I would like to see you in my chambers, immediately."

Raggie and Fred were overjoyed at the decision by the honorable Judge Barlor, and kissed and embraced each other like it was the first and final time.

Driving off to their heavenly paradise, Raggie found complete peace within herself, peace of mind, body, soul and spirit. Free at last, Raggie was free at last, with the one she loved. They had no price on their love, like the Rosemonts.

Prologue

Thirty-five years later, during the Thanksgiving holiday in the city of "Lost Angels"—Los Angeles, California—the God-blessed, innocent, caring son of Freddico and Raggie Jones, named Darrick Price Jones, is about to run into the dreadful, devilish, past of his mother's raging rape, the death-stalking, miserable, haunting nightmare of George Rosemont's cousin, the notorious Mafia funeral boss, Freddieo Rosemont. Darrick's destiny will be shaken by the turmoil that Freddieo Rosemont puts Darrick through, just like the hellish rape nightmares George Rosemont gave Raggie's mind. Only the power of love and God up above will have the final turn of the spinning wheel in the "Wheel of Fortune" in Darrick's life.

Part II

"Stone Love"

One Christmas morning, as the earth was celebrating peace on earth—exactly what Jesus Christ stood for—there was a report of a 150 car pile-up on Interstate 101, the Hollywood Freeway in Hollywood, California, just a few yards from the Rosemont's Funeral Parlor. There were twenty reported dead and approximately fifty injured from the fatal Christmas morning pile-up. This is just one accidental happening that occurred out of about a thousand on Christmas Day nationwide. The American highway is the number one killer in America, the number one cause of death in a nation that is supposed to be an example to the world. America, the world-wide peacemaker, in its own country, on its own grounds, was just the opposite of what it should be. America has the leading cause of death by cigarette and alcohol use, and employs the Democratic government and the nuclear bomb to keep world peace, but by only show of force. Just as the hand gun is supposed to keep the peace. Every police officer has one, yet the murder rate in this country is number one throughout the world. An estimated 20,000 Americans are murdered every year, usually be a hand gun.

On New Year's Eve, there was another report on the radio that a jet plane had just crashed, killing 300 passengers, and a train had derailed, killing 150 passengers. Both the pilot and the train engineer were diagnosed as having too much alcohol to drink. On New Year's Day, the Crips and Bloods, two notorious Los Angeles gangs, had a turf-drug war, shooting each other in South Central Los Angeles, an estimated twenty killed, ten on each side—ten Bloods and ten Crips.

Darrick Price Jones was driving home from work one day and a fire truck just missed his car, going to a neighborhood fire. One died from smoke suffocation, a marijuana dealer who forgot to put out his reefer stick and fell asleep while in a deep high. Darrick always passed by Rosemont's Funeral Parlor everyday going to and from work, noticing at least one car wreck a week, almost in the same spot, a few yards from Rosemont's Funeral Parlor.

One of the Rosemonts happened to work at the same postal facility that Darrick did. He never knew that her relatives owned and operated the Rosemont's Funeral Parlor, the number one parlor in Los Angeles, California, nor did he wonder why there was a car wreck in the same spot every week for the past ten years, just a few yards from Rosemont's Funeral Parlor.

The Rosemonts seemed like nice people from eyesight, when Linda Angelo showed Darrick some of her relatives' photographs at work. He had known Linda for almost ten years. She had started working the same year and month Darrick did. They became close friends, and he even took her out on a couple of dates. He never knew her relatives killed people to keep their business alive. Their funeral parlor business was so famous and profitable in Los Angeles that they even helped the handicapped by donating almost $250,000.00 each year, but he came to find out the truth later during the year, when Linda told Darrick it was just a tax write-off.

Linda was a very well-liked individual, looking like an angel sent from heaven with a smile you would never forget, and hazel-green eyes, about five-feet nine-inches, a few inches shorter than Darrick. To some people she was the sweetest person around or whom you ever wanted to meet. She was always helping people in need, taking up donations when they were sick or in the hospital, especially when there was death in someone else's family, and acting almost as though they were part of her own family. She was very popular, known throughout her neighborhood, city and state. She sang in the church choir, and was very active in neighborhood activities, like raising food for the needy on Thanksgiving Day.

Darrick liked Linda for her kindness, soft-spokeness and glowing-like-the-sunshine personality, something he admired in Linda when they first met. She was taking up money donations for the death of one of the postal employees who had died in a car accident while driving to work. Funny thing, though, the accident happened just a few yards from the Rosemont's Funeral Parlor. The other driver of the car was seriously injured. The employee was also buried by the Rosemont's Funeral Parlor. He never knew Linda was taking up the donations to help the postal employee's relatives pay for the expensive funeral arrangements.

The burial ground, seven feet by seven feet squared off; the burial casket or box made of pine wood; the tuxedo, black with red trim; the renting of the Catholic priest; the white limousine; the sheriff directing traffic; and the private security guards leased by Rosemont's Funeral Parlor for protection against any outbreaks while the "dust to dust, peaceful burial sermon" was in process, were all quite expensive.

Oh, yes, I forgot to mention the parlor's artificial facial fixation of a movie star's face on the dead person's skull, using about a pound of makeup and some more plastic surgery to make a dead person pleasant to look at, usually with an expensive hair wig.

The total cost came to about $20,000, the total of the insurance policy the dead employee carried when hired at the post office. The employee was also not to be buried by an oak tree, but by a pine tree, an additional $500.00 in burial expenses.

The more expensive burials by the Rosemont's cost between thirty and fifty thousand dollars, including a complete orchestra, a gold trim casket, made of silver, with a patterned gold-colored interior, looking heavenly; and a flower assortment with roses, carnations, tulips, wildfire pussy willows—you ask for it, you got it. Some relatives of the deceased could request their favorite singer, such as Michael Jackson or Diana Ross, for an additional ten thousand dollars, if they were available, to go along with the orchestra.

The tombstone and engraving could cost an additional five to ten thousand dollars if the stone was marble, granite or engraved in gold or silver letters, talking about the poor, deceased soul's name. The number of limousines the deceased relatives requested also cost anywhere from one hundred to three hundred dollars per hour. Tuxedo and wedding gowns, fur coats, gold and diamond jewelry, diamonds installed in the lip, nose, ears, fingernails, toenails, or wherever desired by the deceased's relatives also cost additional. The cost could even skyrocket further if all the extras were included, for instance a mini-movie production of the entire burial affair. Sometimes the arrangements for an after-party at the Hilton Hotel or the Holiday Inn was arranged for the distribution of any insurance money leftover from the poor soul's life insurance policy.

So there you have it: Instead of a sad affair, it became a joyous occasion, a celebration as a matter of fact, of a love for death. No tears of sorrow, but tears of laughter and joy. Yes, the Rosemont's Funeral Parlor service was well-known and well-liked by many, especially those who liked the insurance money transactions which were distributed equally amongst the Rosemont's employees, mainly co-caine addicts and alcoholics. Some called this "under the table money," meaning tax free, which was paid out according to how much one contributed to the victim's death. Linda, sometimes called "Proud Mary," for what reason Darrick had not the faintest idea, asked him to help her distribute some funeral parlor leaflets and brochures advertising burial plans and cost. So Darrick did, doing her a favor, not thinking too much about it.

Linda Angelo, the Proud Mary, was also a postal inspector, although nobody knew what her job title was in the entire postal building facility. Her main job was responsibility for the safety of the postal employees, or supposed to have been. No one ever really knew she was the main cause of death among several postal employees. She was mixed racially with Indian, white, black, Hispanic and even Asian-Pacific Oriental, and that probably had a lot to do with her open door burial policy. There was no prejudice, anyone and everyone was welcomed to be buried at her relatives' funeral parlor. The leaflets Darrick passed out for her were very informative, with a payment pay-back plan, loans available, and the total cost of burial, from simple cremation to elaborate, expensive burials.

During his postal career, he never suspected Linda of the numerous deaths at the postal facility. Darrick never knew that by just saying something to a person at the right time could cause one's death or that even a certain way one might look at a person, or inch around a person while he's working on the floor, just happening to get in his way at the right time, could cause the most unbelievable back trouble, heart trouble or a stroke, an asthma attack, or a severe accident, like a foot or hand injury, the limbs you need the most for driving your car to and from work. Instead of seeing who is being unsafe on the work floor, she would see who had a cold or the flu or who was allergic to dust or molds, which were in abundance at the postal facility, or whose blood pressure was too high, all to aggravate their health conditions to make that person sicker than at first. Linda was like the death wish from hell, trying her best to make sure you died, by health failure or car wreck.

Linda's favorite weapon was called "stress." If she could, she would get a person stressed out, or to overreact to any particular situation, especially verbal confrontations, resulting in her final solution, death. For how would a simple, everyday, common postal employee know that someone wanted them dead, by just talking?

For example, "Why are you eating?" asks the supervisor.

One might reply, "I'm not eating, I'm chewing Doublemint chewing gum. Have a stick, please?"

The supervisor might say, "Don't tell me you're not eating; don't hand me that garbage."

The employee might take it the wrong way, thinking, "He is saying I'm chewing garbage," and might say, "I don't chew damned garbage."

The supervisor might say, "You don't use profanity in this building; this is a government facility, and profanity is punishable by administrative action."

But the employee thinks he's pulling his leg, and says, "Who don't say damn in this goddamn building!!"

The supervisor might get hostile at this point, taking advantage of the emotional state of being, and say, "Please don't say anything else," knowing that the employee can't keep his mouth shut at this moment.

The employee shouts, "Who in the hell you telling to shut up! You don't tell me to shut up!"

The supervisor might instruct the employee to perform his job duties, but the employee's too aroused, tenses, and on edge to perform the duties at the moment. He tells the supervisor again that he "can't come over here and tell me I'm eating, call me a liar, and then tell me to start back performing my duties!" Nervousness also may set in at the same time that the employee is tense and aroused, and the attitude that the supervisor just gave him doesn't permit him to perform his duties, degrading his pride, self-respect and ego.

The employee just stares at the supervisor eye to eye until he finally says, "I warn you, get back to work or I'll write you up for something else, like failure to follow instructions."

Now the employee's really pissed, with the build up of the supervisor accusing him of eating, then calling him a liar, telling him to get back to work after he interrupted him while he was working, and finally warning him if he didn't get back to work he would take further administrative action.

So here we have just what was wanted—a nervous, tensed up, aroused, on edge, about to explode individual, that if anyone pushed the wrong way might overreact in the wrong way, and eventually take their life. This has happened time and time again—murder in the first degree without a weapon, only a simple verbal confrontation. Usually at the post office the employee jumps in his car, hits the gas pedal and is going ninety miles per hour down the highway, until somebody slams on the brakes because something fell off a truck hauling trash and the employee runs dead smack into the rear end of the truck, ending up as dead as a doornail in Rosemont's Funeral Parlor.

Yes, stress is a killer that no one realizes exists but Linda, using it to her advantage to get rich. One thing's for sure—working inside a postal facility is about as depressing as working inside a hospital emergency ward. Seeing a person getting ready to die is very depressing for doctors and nursing staff, especially to see someone die in their face after they put out every effort to save that person's life. But to Darrick, it was even more depressing to not see his friends and co-workers who had passed away because of a car accident, pneumonia, ill health aggravated by the working conditions on the job, or a heart attack or asthma attack aggravated by stress from the supervisors who were indirectly paid by Linda for their contribution or fair share of causing an employee's death.

Employees with heart trouble and asthma were given a hard time, usually by stressing them by supervision, activating a stroke or asthma attack. Employees who had to drive far—two to three hours a day, were usually overworked by their supervisors, not to mention driving through the poor highway construction, and especially were overworked on rainy days. Supervisors dished out stress almost simultaneously with the same time it started raining. With no commuter trains, what a perfect opportunity for some more highway deaths. Yes, Los Angeles has the most highways in the nation, and of course, the most funeral parlors and graveyards in the entire nation, most of them right by the highways. Los Angeles' nickname, "The City of the Angels" should be changed to "The City of Funeral Parlor Paradise."

The Rosemonts damn near ran the entire city. They were in politics, real estate, highway and transportation development, city development, the gambling casino business, investors in the entertainment business and other prospective profitable businesses, not to mention murder and dope dealing. The Rosemonts were tied together by a number of other smaller funeral parlors, assisting them by any means necessary. Their politicians made sure the transportation system didn't build any more commuter trains after the RTD had brought the red car commuter train system, so as not to hinder their funeral parlor business in any way, fashion, or form; knowing the majority of their business came from highway car fatalities of hard American workers like Darrick, who were trying to earn a living.

Their politicians also made sure that a person had a right to die, and alcohol stores were everywhere and open seven days a week, only closing four hours during a twenty-four hour period, from two A.M. to six A.M. In South Central Los Angeles, there is a liquor store on every fucking corner, and one can purchase liquor at the gas stations even, or at the grocery store, and especially at all the Seven-Eleven stores all over the state.

They, the politicians, made damned sure that cigarettes were also available twenty-four hours, 365 days a year, at all gas stations and twenty-four hour grocery markets. Cancer, being the number one killer in American, can be caused just from inhaling the carbon monoxide, along with smog and air pollution, and these alone are enough to kill anyone just sitting next to someone who is blowing the shit out of their mouth and nostrils, or they might cause an asthma attack if you so happened to be asthmatic or have some other chronic lung condition.

The politicians also made absolutely sure that affordable homes were no less then one hour's drive each way on the deadly, congested highways. More affordable homes, those a little less expensive, were farther, one-and-a-half hours each way on the smoggiest, deadliest highways in the nation.

So the funeral parlor business was bringing in the sheep, or the dead, at an unbelievable burial rate. To live to be twenty years of age in Los Angeles, California, was almost a miracle, especially if one lived in South Los Angeles, where gang warfare was a vast and daily rampant activity. The hound of death knocked at every child's door in the "Valley of Death," the Funeral Paradise City of graveyards, Los Angeles, California. The Rosemonts buried at will and people paid the price to get buried, looking pretty like a movie star, by devils in disguise, the Rosemonts. The funeral proceedings arranged by the Rosemonts seemed like a satanic gathering by a group of hell praisers.

Los Angeles, California, was the home of movie stars, the entertainment capital of the world, with all the music recording studios and a huge sign that said, "Hollywood" spread across a mountain top that somehow suckered in more people to its location than any other tourist attraction in America. California, with its warm climate, had more of a population than any other state, almost 30 million people.

With this many people in one state, private security was in abundant demand. Most apartments in Los Angeles were security buildings, and most of the houses had iron bars across the windows and doors for added protection against burglars or whatever threatens one's peace of mind. If one could afford more security, like alarm systems or even patrolled security, it was purchased. The city of Los Angeles was in a complete state of paranoia, with people afraid to go out at night because of being a possible victim of crime. The whole entire city was taken over by the hounds of death, the funeral parlor Mafia, but how was Darrick to know he was on the top of the list in Linda's private funeral parlor book.

Darrick, a considerate, soft-spoken individual, a Christian believing in God Almighty, followed the Bible like all Christians. Darrick was as innocent as a lamb, always helping other people out in whatever way possible. Linda took advantage of his kindness, wholeheartedness, and soft, gentle personality. To Linda, Darrick was money in the bank. Linda investigated his life insurance policy that would be rewarded to his younger sister as the beneficiary, and he had taken out the maximum amount of $250,000.

Linda knew she could convince his sister to have him buried in her relatives' funeral parlor. Linda also investigated Darrick's health background to see if he had any chronic illness or diseases, or if his mother or father or their relatives had any hereditary diseases. Linda, being an inspector for the post office, could do so or was authorized to investigate Darrick for her benefit. Linda even checked Darrick's dental records to see when he might need dental service, maybe for a possible toothache. Linda so happened to enjoy seeing people dead, and of course, in pain. Linda also most definitely checked Darrick's financial background, including his friends and relatives, to make sure, when the time was right for him to die, Darrick would be broke and have no access to any money to use for transportation, gas or for getting away from his overdue death.

Linda quite naturally checked her victim's diet and sleeping habits, and loved to see her victims burned out, completely exhausted and hungry, having no energy to put up any resistance. But mostly, Linda checked her victim's drug consumption, always calculating the worst possibility before they dried out, either a car accident, a fatal shooting, or an overdose of drugs, of course. Linda would always sleep with her victim to see how much wind they had stored in their lungs, knowing perfectly well when they might run out of breath if any confrontation arose, like chasing a motherfucker down the street, shooting bullets at his ass.

Although Los Angeles has more graveyards than a war zone, it might have to do with the Rosemont's and Linda's freakish, strange sex habits, like anal oral sex and getting sexual climaxes from dead bodies, because their penises wouldn't go soft or flat, staying hard all the time. Linda kept her strange sex habits secret, so as not to alarm her male and female sex partners. Linda had just about everyone at the post office sewed up, and she had the right to their burial when they were dead, all except Darrick.

Linda decided to make Darrick her main lover, since he didn't believe in burials. Maybe she could change his mind to compensate for her needs, for whenever Linda was in need, she would have a co-worker of hers buried by her relatives, at the Rosemont's Funeral Parlor.

First, of course, she would have them killed, making it look like an accident or a natural death due to a chronic health condition, especially those with heart conditions and lung conditions like asthma. For those with asthma, she would simply find out what triggered their asthma, like if one was allergic to pollen or bees, she simply made sure they would get an ample supply of pollen or bee stings until death. Sometimes stress would cause frequent asthma attacks. Stress most definitely favored co-workers who were overweight or who smoked and drank a lot, causing severe heart attacks if they already had heart ailments, and of course, high blood pressure.

Linda directed death in the postal facility like a movie director directing actors and actresses for a new motion picture by Paramount. Linda trained each and every supervisor in how to stress and become a stressor, causing a stress plague among common postal co-workers. Tension built up to the maximum, causing a deadly stroke every month. Funeral notices were posted on the bulletin boards for all to see, to build up interest in her relatives' funeral parlor business, hoping to get everyone to attend this depressing monthly affair of burying the dead, who always looked like a movie star when the Rosemont's Funeral Parlor beauticians finished with their plastic surgery and overall makeup.

Darrick was fucking with "Proud Mary" Linda's ego and pride, and she was determined to get Darrick to sign a pre-burial contract with the Rosemont's Funeral Parlor before his unfortunate death due to natural causes, or a sudden act of

God, like everybody else who worked at the post office with Linda. Although Linda's relatives were the Rosemonts, her full name was Linda Smith Angelo, and Darrick's full name was Darrick Price Jones, and Linda had the right burial price for him.

Linda had a twin sister named Sally Angelo, nicknamed, "Fast Sally Ann." She also worked at the post office, but in management, and nobody on the work floor knew Sally existed except for the personnel in management, who were not located at all near the work floor, but completely out of sight from everybody except management, who had a secret code to enter the door in the management area. From the management area, they viewed the work floor by closed circuit television monitors to count the volume of mail for each different work shift, or were supposed to have, anyway.

But sometimes, Sally viewed closely the employees on Linda's hit list, taking notes of their weaknesses, what made them sick, nervous, upset, get on edge, stressed, or tensed, or whether they were overworked, tired, did not get any sleep, had recent problems or worries at home, or death among their relatives. Even illness in the family or amongst their relatives, Linda was curious to find out, using it to her advantage to bury her clients so no one would suspect foul play or murder.

Her relatives in real estate would make absolutely sure that the postal employees would buy a house far out, at least one hour or more each way to and from work, with the house made of glued sawdust and glued one-quarter-inch thick cement, that if caught afire would go up like a match box with no time to escape, if a person was inside sleeping, or on the toilet bowl.

With a postal employee's salary, that was all that one could afford as a house, which was not even made of wood or lumber, but of sawdust glued together pasted with about one-fourth of an inch of glued cement, located outside of Los Angeles, near the largest earthquake fault in the country in San Bernardino County. Or out in the Mojave Desert, where every company has tried to use the desert as a toxic waste dump. They had a high cancer rate amongst their children out there because of buried toxic waste not yet discovered. With the backing of their politicians, cheaply built real estate and poor commuter transportation system, Los Angeles was a "Funeral Parlor Paradise."

Linda had the idea of getting Darrick to maybe buy or lease some real estate out near San Bernardino's earthquake fault or Mojave Desert toxic waste dump sites, hoping he would get burned out from the long driving and eventually have a deadly car accident like all the other damned fools.

But first, she had to get him to sign a pre-burial contract with the Rosemonts, since his life insurance policy was so appetizing, $250,000 for his little sister, Darlene Price. She was just about to turn the age of eighteen. Only Darlene Price Jones would get the $250,000 upon Darrick's unforeseen death, be it natural, accidental or by an act of God. With Darrick's life insurance policy, his sister Darlene could afford a two-or three-bedroom house, even within the city limits of Los Angeles, California.

Yes, the average house in Los Angeles cost $250,000 and wasn't even made of lumber. The only affordable housing on Darrick's income was out of city limits, one-and-a-half hours to drive each way, costing anywhere from $80,000 to $120,000 with closing costs, and the average mortgage payment $900 to $1,200 a month and it wasn't even made out of lumber. A postal employee's salary was near the cost of living in Los Angeles, or just enough to maintain some standard of living besides becoming homeless.

And please don't mention property taxes—heaven forbid, they are outrageous. Some property taxes were an extra $100 to $300 a month. Add that to the mortgage payment and baby, people were looking for aluminum cans to recycle and all the overtime they could get their hands on. It so happened that the property taxes rose with the union contract pay raise; every three years the union and Postal Board of Governors negotiated a new contract, leaving employees in the same living conditions as before. The same standard of living always persisted—not homeless yet, just poor!

Darrick never wondered why some of his co-workers wore the same clothing every damned day, making Darrick's life more depressing, as he worked in a dull, gray-painted, dusty, noisy, virus-plagued, tense, and stressful motherfucking post office facility five days a week. There were all these contributing factors, with number one being having a low income in a city of movie stars who got $35,000 for one damned commercial in which they said an almost complete sentence like, "Wear blue, blue jeans pants, baby," which is Darrick's yearly salary.

The other contributing factor was his place of residence, which was three hours on the highway every day, so he had to take No-Doz 100 percent caffeine tablets every other hour at work and every hour on the highway, as he tried to stay awake with the damned smog and air pollution blinding his ass, usually just missing death. Darrick always slammed on the brakes just in the nick of time. Death on the highway had become an everyday game to Darrick, who saw an occasional car accident, wondering when it might be his turn but never wondering if the car accident was fatal, because Darrick didn't give a damn, just wanted to get the fuck off the highway as soon as possible.

So, after leaving his glued-together house, and arriving at work from the deadly highway, he entered Linda's funeral parlor paradise monopoly, the post office, where she took turns spinning the wheel of death for her next victim. He walked to his assigned work area on the work floor, with dust crystals hanging over his head and his co-worker coughing in his face, holding a tissue full of mucus, saying, "How's it going?" Of course, Darrick looked at him like a goddamned fool because the son-of-a-bitch wore the same damned clothes every day, with a foul odor to go along with it. Before Darrick could get his breath, he told Darrick another one of his friends just passed away last week from pneumonia.

Darrick, not believing what he said, was about to fall asleep from the exhaustion of being overworked and under-rested, said, "Where is the funeral notice?" And Linda came strolling by, swaying her hips, and calling Darrick's name out loud. This was the month of November, the month to be thankful for, with Thanksgiving around the corner. Linda wanted to invite Darrick to the funeral to ride with her in her relatives' limousine and also to her family's Thanksgiving dinner. Darrick didn't like funerals, believing they were actually seances for devilish people trying to bring back the dead to life, and believed people should not be buried anyway, but only cremated.

Darrick believed that funeral parlors were for fools who wanted to look pretty and be dressed in the latest style for their relatives and friends before leaving the earth, to be buried six feet under the earth, with peace of mind and finally having that heaven or hell, and leaving memories of looking good while on earth. They wanted buried in the best clothing and wearing the finest jewelry, to be driven in the classiest of automobiles, a chauffeur-driven white Cadillac limousine, and be buried in a casket made of silver and gold, with the letters of their last name engraved in gold on an expensive stone, the finest the earth had to offer, perhaps marble or granite, placed over their artificially embalmed, plastic, facial surgery repaired dead ass, all for a costly "bill" from the finest, freakiest motherfuckers living, the Rosemonts.

Darrick didn't want to hurt Linda's feelings, her being the kind, sweet, person he thought she was, and he told her he would love to have Thanksgiving dinner with her and her relatives, but that he had a doctor's appointment the day of the funeral for his unfortunate dead co-worker.

Thanksgiving Day rolled around, and Darrick was eager to have dinner with Linda and meet her relatives, the Rosemonts. Darrick arrived at Linda's apartment in Los Angeles on Thanksgiving Day, the busiest day of the year as far as highway traffic was concerned. But Darrick took a few side streets not too many people knew about, missing all the holiday highway traffic. Linda greeted him with a kiss on his cheek, dressed in a mini, red hot lamb dress, with black lamb boots to her knees, and a loudly colored yellow blouse almost showing her breast, cut real low, with a black lamb cap to match her boots, and wearing a red lamb jacket to match her dress. Darrick had dressed plain and simply, in a black wool suit, white shirt and black tie, and a black leather jacket. They both jumped into Darrick's 1990 black Ford Mustang GT five-speed, and Linda told Darrick the directions on the way to her relatives' house, a fifteen minute drive from her apartment.

They arrived at the lush mansion sitting on top of Belair Mountain overlooking Los Angeles, on the side of a steep cliff, with a private driveway to the entrance of the Rosemont's mansion with about fifteen acres of green grass. The three-story mansion, built of white marble, was surrounded by ten pine trees. Outside sat two Rolls Royce late model cars, painted gold. A white fountain stood out in front, shooting water almost twenty feet high from the ground.

Darrick was somewhat surprised at the amazing wealth before his very eyes, but not really, because Linda already told him her relatives were very wealthy. Linda told Darrick to blow his car horn twice, after parking behind one of the gold Rolls Royces. Linda's twin sister, Sally, came running out of the mansion, yelling, "Linda, Linda, Linda!!!" They kissed each other on the lips, as Linda introduced her twin sister to Darrick. The only way he could tell them apart was from the different clothing they each had on. They were identical twins, and Darrick had never seen twins look so exactly alike before in his life—the same height, weight, body build, hair color, color of eyes, and facial looks—they even sounded alike talking to each other.

Darrick wondered if Linda or Sally had ever flipped out while looking directly at each other, wondering, "Are you me or am I you?" Darrick slowly walked with the twins to the entrance of the mansion, and went in. He almost fainted from looking at an entire family of strange, vulture-looking, weird motherfuckers, who looked almost alike, with the only noticeable difference being their height and weight. "Yes, sir," Darrick was thinking to himself, "this is definitely not the Adams' family, but the Rosemont family, and which family is the strangest is a complete mystery."

Damn near spooked to death, he started to shiver, his knees shaking, and almost shit and pissed on himself at the same time, realizing that he seemed to be on the edge of death in a mansion on top of a mountain, damn near hanging on a cliff, full of none other than a house seemingly full of incest freaks, looking like a bunch of funeral vultures that he had never seen before in his life. They all stared at Darrick as if he was the Thanksgiving dinner.

Linda introduced Darrick to her relatives, saying out loud, "Here's my guest, Darrick Price Jones!"

They all said, "How earthly pleasant to meet you," all at the same time in such a haunting spookish tone that Darrick almost started to run back to his car, but looking at Linda in her mini-dress, changed his mind instantly. Darrick gained back his courage and stated he was pleased to meet Linda's relatives, the Rosemonts. He was amazed at the furniture, all of it looking in some way like funeral caskets, and the walls were painted dark gray, giving Darrick a haunted feeling of being stalked and finally suckered into the dungeon of the hounds of death, all lurking for his blood, ready to shake inside his soul until he turned into a corpse's shell.

Darrick was only trying to please Linda in staying for Thanksgiving dinner, although not really hungry anymore, his appetite vanishing. Linda showed him through the halls of the mansion, which looked like a museum for the dead. Darrick felt more and more out of place. The paintings displayed on the wall of the Rosemonts' all had the same smile and staring eyes, and spooked Darrick even more, giving him gastrointestinal problems, so his stomach started growling and making strange noises.

Linda thought Darrick was really hungry and couldn't wait to eat, hearing his stomach growling from time to time as they were strolling through the mansion's hallways, waiting for dinner to be served. Finally they came to a portrait painting of Linda hanging on the wall, almost life-size, under a starry crystal light fixture hanging from the ceiling. Darrick slowly smiled, looking at the painting of Linda, and asked her, not trying to be funny at all, "Is that you or your twin sister?" Linda smiled at Darrick, staring into his eyes like he had never seen her do before, inched close to him, and finally softly kissing him on the lips. Darrick responded with an intimate kiss, lasting for about one whole minute, not realizing he was kissing the face of death. Releasing his lips from hers, a silence came between them, neither one taking their eyes off of the other's.

Darrick broke the silent spell, saying, "Well, wasn't that delightful. Your lips are so sweet, and your body so tender and warm, how can I bear to be without you in my life now? I've always liked you and you probably already knew it. But I did not really want to try and get serious with you because of the disappointment I can't accept if you were to deny me the once in a lifetime opportunity to love you."

Linda spoke hesitantly and somewhat nervously, saying, "I wouldn't dare deny you the opportunity, for I always had you on my mind."

All along in the spacious hallway, they kissed and embraced each other sensuously for the first time, as if it was the last time. Petting came into play and Linda, catching herself before matters got out of hand, said, "Let's continue this after dinner at my place. Maybe you might want to spend the night, since you have such a long drive home and the holiday traffic is murderous. It's almost suicidal to drive this time of year."

Darrick, unbelievingly shocked, but pleased to have heard what was offered by her, said, "Yes, you're absolutely right. I almost had an accident on the way to your place today, but I guess the Lord was on my side this time. I missed slamming into the back of a car that was parked in the middle of the highway with the engine hood up. I guess the car had engine trouble or ran out of gas or something. I'm glad you invited me to spend the night. You know every time I drive on the highway, it seems like I'm going through a slaughter house for cows. I'm so tired of seeing people killed and hurt from car accidents. I pass by almost three car accidents a week, thinking maybe that could have been me. Sometimes I get depressed just thinking I have to drive on the highway just to get to work, since there are no commuter trains or buses of any kind out where I live."

Linda, showing her feelings for Darrick, said, "I know how you must feel, baby. That's why my relatives are so wealthy—car accidents are the number one killer in this country and especially in Los Angeles and California. They asked me to help their funeral parlor business by having my co-workers on the job sign a pre-burial contract arrangement plan that you helped me hand out at work.

The maid rang the dinner bells and Linda told Darrick dinner was ready. They joined the rest of Linda's relatives, the Rosemonts and Angelos, at the very long dining table that seated approximately thirty dinner guests. The elaborate dinner table setting had real silver spoons, forks, and knives, and the dinner plates were gold trimmed as was the crystal glassware, with glowing white candlesticks set in gold fixtures just for the candles. Hanging above the table, chained from the ceiling, was a huge crystal light fixture, sparkling like diamonds. The Rosemonts all smiled, with the reflection of the crystal light fixture sparkling like diamonds in their eyes, all looking at Darrick.

The lights were dimmed on the huge crystal light fixture and the Rosemont's and Angelo's shadows were cast against the dull gray wall, making the whole scene look ghostly. The maid lit the candles, making everything a bit brighter and somewhat romantic, as Darrick and Linda were seated next to each other by the maid. Everybody was seated, about thirty blood relatives of some kind or another, now with fiery diamonds glowing in their eyes reflecting from the crystal and candlelight. To Darrick, they started looking like fiery, diamond-sparkle-eyed vultures in all black dress attire, like they were ready for a seance of some kind. Never before in Darrick's life had he seen such devilish looking people, all dressed in black with white lace trimming.

Mr. Freddieo Rosemont was sitting at the head of the table with Mrs. Rosemont at the opposite end, and announced a blessing for Thanksgiving Day. Darrick could barely hear the blessing that sounded like a brief sermon, and then the turkey was served, with dressing topped with marshmallows, golden brown and crisp, a large bowl of fruit punch, tossed salad, green string beans, cranberry sauce, assorted cakes and pies, and a complimentary bar with assorted brands of alcohol—wines, liquors, beers, brandies, you name it, it was available. Darrick had a full helping of each dish, especially the turkey and dressing. There was casual conversation amongst the relatives while orchestra music played over the intercom system, a very relaxing music and very enjoyable to listen to while having a delicious Thanksgiving dinner.

To Darrick, the whole dinner arrangement was splendid, and he was more relaxed, now somewhat feeling comfortable talking about the pleasant weather they were having. He was finishing supper when he suddenly, with extreme difficulty, tried to catch his breath, and fell face first into his dinner plate, having an asthma attack on Thanksgiving Day. He finally fainted to the floor, and while Linda ran to the phone to call an ambulance, the other guests and relatives panicked. Darrick was spoiling a pleasant dinner and such a pleasant day of all days, Thanksgiving Day.

Mr. Freddieo Rosemont bent down over Darrick, listening for a heart beat, feeling for a pulse, hoping he was dead, because to Mr. F. Rosemont, he was nothing more than money in the bank, someone Linda suckered into coming over for dinner, like all the time. The overloaded turkey dressing was full of tranquilizers and somewhat over salted, but Darrick had not been able to tell because of the spicy gravy on top of the dressing.

This was a for-sure burial, thought Mr. F. Rosemont, smiling, seeing no life left in him. Linda came running back to Darrick, wiped the food from his face with a tablecloth and struck him as hard as she could with her fist balled up over his heart, the other hand opening his mouth, as she was blowing her lungs out, trying to revive his breathing. Mr. F. Rosemont's other relatives stood watching, looking like their favorite dessert was about to be served—death. The Rosemonts had a love for death, with their tongues hanging out their mouths, ready to suck the blood out of Darrick like haunting vultures.

But Linda shouted, "Stay back, he's mine!" The Rosemonts were closing in like a bunch of hungry vultures for the kill. Darrick's eyelids started coming open and his breathing finally came back, as he asked Linda what happened in a weak, soft voice. The ambulance arrived, the paramedics entered, and then Darrick and Linda were off to the hospital, Linda falling in love with him.

Meanwhile, the Rosemonts were furiously angry that they didn't get the opportunity to actually suck the blood out of Darrick's dead body and have an orgy celebrating Darrick's death, seeing as that was why they all looked so much alike in the first, from having sex amongst themselves—yes, incest.

Mr. F. Rosemont and a few of his relatives went to the television studios they rented every day to view their Rosemont graveyard burial ground to see if any dead bodies had escaped the death hole, to watch their prospective victims in the deadly highway traffic, and to get Los Angeles city gangs, the Bloods and Crips to do some drive-by shooting. They also tuned in to the post office to see if any of their pre-signed funeral burial contract suckers were ready to have a stroke or asthma attack, such as Darrick had or to check if one had just come from the doctor's office after being treated for high blood pressure or a cold or flu. They would then aggravate the conditions around that one to cause a possible stroke if the person was seen for high blood pressure, possibly using a stressor to cause lots of loud banging and loud noises to get the person very tensed, or even have a supervisor ask him if he was eating when he was chewing gum, or even accuse the person of saying something or of having done something they knew nothing about.

If the person just had a cold or flu, they would have a person who is just starting to show signs of a cold start coughing next to the other, trying to cause a reoccurrence of the cold or flu. The Rosemont Funeral Parlor personnel caused more deaths than any Los Angeles city gang, heavy traffic, flu, disease, hand gun or other deadly weapon, just by the use of stress psychology mastered by Freddieo Rosemont, and his personnel at the television studios, with the use of radar sound technology.

By the use of stress psychology by a third person in the television studios, they could make a first and second person go against each other or do each other in by killing or assault and battery, arguing over nothing, and finally carrying it over to the public, traffic and household. They would carry the temperament from being stressed at work to the general public, to the family household, and maybe cause a traffic accident, or perpetrate assault and battery on their spouse or even children by child abuse.

Voice imitation is the key element by the third person, usually done by sophisticated radar sound technology such as having the first or second person think the other said something they actually didn't say, but the third person did by imitating the first or second person, and by using the radar in the television studios, they could cause a conflict or confrontation of some kind. They wanted to bring about the end result, a confrontation or conflict of some kind, preferably death, because the Rosemonts had a love for death.

The Rosemonts seemed like the Devil in disguise, howling throughout the day and night like the hounds of hell to shake inside a corpse shell and within the soul, haunting the very innocent like the death plague of Satan. They had no mercy on child, woman or man; no one was safe from the Rosemonts' evil spell cast upon the Los Angeles public like bloodthirsty vultures loving every drop of blood of a dead body.

People were dying innocently like lambs, not knowing why someone would come in a postal facility and start shooting everyone in sight, finally killing themselves to make the Rosemont's Funeral Parlor have the perfect take. They didn't know why a postal employee would go home and start shooting up their entire family, or why a gang would drive by and start shooting bullets at people on a public sidewalk in downtown Los Angeles at the peak of rush hour. Causing death and bringing in the dead was the Rosemonts' business, and how in the hell could they go out of business with the irritating motherfuckers causing everything from heart attacks to death.

Linda had brought her relatives at the Rosemont's Funeral Parlor many a burned out, overworked, stressed out, over-reacting, high blood-pressured, heart-troubled and asthmatic clientele before in the past, but Darrick was something special to Linda. She had never before saved anyone's life, especially at her relatives' mansion. Something must have come over her, like maybe actually falling in love with Darrick, whom she originally intended to have her relatives bury.

At the hospital, Darrick was given an asthmatic treatment, something to breathe that cleared up his lungs and something to cleanse his stomach. Linda was by Darrick's side every second, not letting him out of her sight. Upon Darrick's release from the hospital, Linda drove his car and him to her apartment, where Darrick would be spending the night with Linda until he felt better and stronger. Then came the fascination of them love rocking around the clock, giving each other the best of what they got. The whole-hearted lovemaking poured out of each other's soul until they were finally exhausted, and fell asleep in each other's arms.

Linda and Darrick were in love with each other for sure; a long way from gone in the wind, but just starting that burning flame in each other's soul. They were holding the keys to each other's lives in possessing each other with a lusting body chemistry like never before, the ultimate in love, and they had reached a total climax of lovemaking, wanting possession of each other forever. Their secret, private, and sincere vows of their divine love were made; a unity making them both one individual, never to turn against the other, to always respect and love the other, no matter what happened, through tough times or easy times, no matter how long they lasted. Through hell or heaven, rain, snow or hail, misery, pain, or joy, they vowed to always love each other, to meet each other all the way, no matter what, in a forever true love, in the high life or in the low life. They belonged to each other, deciding to go through life together with their souls free as the birds flying in the sky.

Linda couldn't let the Rosemonts have Darrick like the others she usually brought for their supper; the Rosemonts vulturing blood from human corpses, nourishing themselves like a bunch of batty vampires, then burying bodies in gold clothing and silver footwear and even implanting gold dentures if the buried soul's relatives so desired. The Rosemonts got a double treat of the fulfillment of blood drinking and the burial profit money that was their reward and motivation. They had a sick desire to bury as many people as they could, loving every bit of death.

Linda and Darrick came to the conclusion that the dinner must have been too spicy for Darrick, making him think he had a food allergy. Although Linda knew better, she did not dare reveal the secrets of death of her relatives, the Rosemonts, to Darrick, for fear Darrick might become vengeful and try to get even with the Rosemonts and also break up with her. This she didn't want: to bear the heartache and hurt of love. Memories of making love to Darrick she couldn't handle if Darrick suddenly stopped loving her because of her bloodthirsty relatives calculating Darrick's death and Darrick wanting that revenge.

Linda had felt her body melt within Darrick's arms, and did not want to lose this ecstasy of love. Darrick told Linda he was going to have a physical examination to see if there were other health complications developing with his age, now thirty-five, with Linda only thirty. Darrick was now fully rested enough to drive home, an hour's drive from Linda's place.

How long Linda and Darrick would stay together, only time would tell. Now that Darrick's world was no longer lonely, he just wanted to please and be with his new-found love. Linda had come into Darrick's world—what more could he ask for? Darrick had found his heaven on earth, his final destiny—Linda. She was on his mind all the time, like the hands of a clock with the second hand ticking away, and every second Linda was in Darrick's mind. He wanted to be back beside Linda as soon as he left her apartment, and was driving home on the highway. Linda stayed at home, finally by herself, missing Darrick, who had just left only thirty minutes ago.

The telephone rang and it was her Uncle Freddieo Rosemont, the owner of the funeral parlor, demanding an explanation for saving one of his burial victims. He stated to her that she had ruined the whole Thanksgiving party, and reminded Linda of the good old blood-sucking and orgy days, trying to bring back memories of how good it used to be, and referring to the freakish sex habits they both had in common—the oral-anal and oral sex practices—along with the sucking of a dead corpse's blood to liven up their spirits while in the mood of a free-for-all incest orgy.

Linda, afraid of her uncle's power and influence, said she was sorry, but wanted Darrick all to herself and finally explained that she had fallen in love with him. Her uncle, angry, told her that falling in love with a commoner—a postal employee—was forbidden, and that their relationship should be halted and never should have been developed in the first place. He even went so far as to tell Linda that the next time she saw or had an affair with Darrick, he would be killed immediately. Falling in love was forbidden to her and only a love for death was permitted.

Linda hung up the phone, almost breaking the receiver by slamming it hard, and was heartbroken, in a state of shock from her uncle telling her that to love somebody was forbidden and only loving death was permitted. Time stood still. Linda wanted to rebel against her uncle's demands and wishes, but was frightened at what the outcome might bring. She contemplated, counting the hours, how she and Darrick could keep their new-found love affair alive, without endangering him.

Realizing how much she loved Darrick, she had instantly developed a hate for death and for her uncle's wishes and demands. Linda's behavioral attitude, her attitude about death, was changing to the opposite direction now that she found her first real love. She wanted to escape the hounds of hell looking for death with every chance they got. Their world of death she no longer accepted, or their freakish sex orgies, and blood-sucking their victim's dead corpse until the savage vultures of death had satisfied their hunger cravings for being thirsty for another's dead human blood. The taste of blood to them was like the taste of honey to a bee; being deprived of it was not to be accepted.

Linda knew her uncle watched her like a hawk from the television studios. With the mental conditioning in all of her relatives, they knew that in not obeying the laws of Freddieo Rosemont's rules of death, they would be erased, crucified by the F. Rosemont kingdom killers. The kingdom killers delivered death to those who were condemned by the throne ruled by Linda's uncle, Mr. Freddieo Rosemont, founder of the kingdom of death, a network of funeral parlors all across the state of California and the nation, faithfully conforming to Rosemont's laws of death.

This funeral parlor Mafia, headed by Mr. F. Rosemont, ruled with the hand of Satan, howling like the hounds of hell throughout the day and night across the nation, having no mercy on any man, woman, or child, killing at will with the force of a fire storm, unstoppable. Not even the rains from heaven could halt the evil force of the overpowering death plague the entire nation bore. It was chilling, this wheeling and dealing human bodies to nourish the earth's fertile soil, as Mr. F. Rosemont thought, helping trees grow taller and grass turn greener. This deeply embedded sick thought he kept to himself, also thinking that he was the earth's savior, a god.

Linda, a prisoner of this mad man, wanted no more of his disarranged world, and asked the Lord and Jesus Christ for the guidance to peace of mind and freedom.

"To be strong and to believe in what is right and do the right thing," was the utmost righteous answer she thought the Lord and Jesus Christ delivered as the right guidance to her peace of mind and freedom. First, Linda had to get the fear of death out of her mind, as only God would summon her body and soul at the chosen time. The threats of being condemned by her uncle and of Darrick being killed completely left her train of thought, as she promised herself that if her Uncle Freddieo Rosemont did kill her first and only real true love, Darrick, she would revenge his death until death took her. She no longer accepted, respected or desired her uncle's demands and wishes. Linda decided to reveal her uncle's funeral parlor operations to Darrick for his own safety and protection.

Darrick, just arriving home, heard the phone ringing. It was Linda. Darrick explained to Linda that he had just gotten home when he heard the phone ringing. Linda hysterically but very seriously told Darrick that her uncle threatened to kill him if he was seen with her again, and that the dinner had been loaded with tranquilizers and was supposed to cause an asthmatic attack to kill him. Finally she told him the truth, that she had saved him because she really loved him and he was the first person she ever fell in love with.

She told Darrick not to try to get even or do anything stupid that might get him killed, mentioning that her uncle was the head of an organized syndicated crime network called the funeral parlor Mafia and ruled over a group of kingdom killers who killed at his command, bringing the dead bodies to be buried by his funeral parlor to make him and his organization richer, stronger and unstoppable. He was a cruel ruler of the land, using television studios and radar sound technology.

This radar, she explained, sent signals, imitating others, and used Freddieo's unstoppable stress psychology strategy methods and his knowledge of altering the mind chemistry with tranquilizers, cigarettes, alcohol, marijuana, cocaine, and even sweets and salt, to cause heart attacks, asthma attacks or sudden death. Sometimes tension and over-reacting by his stalked victims who were stressed out carried over day by day until a buildup of anxiety and uncontrollable behavior was developed and the victim was about to explode.

The individual usually had a car accident, because they were tensed at the steering wheel and over-reacting to the flow of traffic, usually by speeding or taking risky chances, like trying to beat a yellow light before it turned red at a traffic light, about to see that apple pie in the sky. Although it was notable to beat the changing colors of the traffic light, they usually ended up another fatality of a car accident. At home or on the job, the unstoppable, berserk madness might possess their total being, and before they realized it, they had killed their whole damned family, the ones they loved the most. Because of over-reacting, and not being themselves, they become mad men, picking up a hand gun, loading it and shooting, shooting, shooting until everybody was dead around them. Suddenly they might realize what they have done and shoot themselves in the forehead, the only way they can forgive themselves.

On the job, they were stressed out by the supervisor because he might have falsely accused them of eating while actually they were chewing Doublemint gum, and an argument developed, then the threat of having their bread-and-butter job taken, over something as stupid as chewing Doublemint gum. Or on the opposite hand, they might take it out on their co-workers, the supervisor constantly harassing them and stressing them for no reason under the sun that they can think of; day by day it carried over to a total buildup of tension, making them on edge about everything, not realizing they had started taking the constant harassment and stressing out on their co-workers, like not speaking anymore like they used to; and go from being sociable to complete solitude, on edge even when someone touched them accidentally; ready to fight or curse a person out, using profanity like they never had before, becoming another person altogether.

One day the supervisor hands them a letter, stating they have a two-week suspension for chewing gum but they need the money to pay for the house note or monthly rent or car note, utility bills, or even to buy food. They would start feeling like the whole world is against them, a complete outcast. They thought their co-workers and especially the supervisor all went against them; they can't take this type of cruelty and disciplinary action dished out by the supervisor. So now with this letter, the icing on the cake, they brought their hand gun to the job site and started shooting everybody in sight, saving the last bullet for themselves like a person possessed by the devil.

The Rosemonts viewed all this action from the television booth, connected to the work site by closed-circuit cable television, cheering the victim on while they are shooting people like they were hired by them, like one of their kingdom killers. The Rosemonts meanwhile calculated the burial cost of each one they killed for them, including possible additional expenses like gold teeth implanted by one of the dead victim's relatives because they didn't know what to do with all the life insurance money when the wheel of fortune happens to turn in their behalf, killing their co-workers.

"Yes," sighed Linda, "my Uncle F. Rosemont knows how to use that key element, stress psychology, to the ultimate to bring in dead bodies left and right, twenty-four hours around the clock, nationwide. So, Darrick, I don't know what else to do, but to warn you, and I love you so much."

Darrick did not want to believe any of this telephone conversation that Linda had just bravely discussed about a "code of silence" to be sworn to and kept amongst herself and her relatives, and if they broke the "code of silence," death was automatically given by the kingdom killers, ordered by her Uncle F. Rosemont.

Linda told Darrick not to reveal any of this conversation to anybody; that if it was found out that she had told him about the funeral parlor Mafia, they would be killed by the kingdom killers. Darrick promised Linda he wouldn't tell anyone and that he would keep it a secret until death. He said good-bye to Linda, then went into deep meditation, contemplating how in the hell she could allow a sick son-of-a-bitch like her Uncle F. Rosemont to run her life. Why Linda must be living amongst a bunch of killers, thought Darrick, like the kingdom killers.

He loved Linda so much, he couldn't allow this to exist, this funeral parlor Mafia, as she called it. Darrick decided to warn the other postal employees of its existence, to have them drop their pre-burial contracts with the Rosemont's Funeral Parlor, and to make higher authorities aware, like the FBI. Getting the Rosemonts out of business was the only way to stop Linda's Uncle F. Rosemont from running her life. Why, Linda must have been frightened damn near to death of her uncle, like a slave with a master named Satan.

But in Freddieo Rosemont's point of view, he was god to Mother Earth, the savior of the planet Earth. He was saving the earth from the humans eating away at all the earth's minerals; from polluting the earth's water supply, its oceans, lakes and rivers; polluting the air; from destroying its rain forests, mountains, valleys and plains.

The humans, to Freddieo Rosemont, were the germs of a virus that were overpopulating the surface of the earth, plagued with diseases like AIDS and other uncontrollable viruses mankind thought it could and had mastered. In Freddieo Rosemont's eyes, the earth would eventually be destroyed by mankind from over-population and from wasting away of the earth's air, water, and natural mineral supply, such as its rain forests, mountains, plains and valleys, since most of the minerals such as diamonds, gold, silver, coal, marble and stone came from the earth's mountains, and other natural minerals came from the plains and valleys, like fertile soil, sand, clay, cement and numerous other minerals. All these earth-given, blessed resources—the air, water and natural minerals from the earth—were being eaten away by humans who had turned into a gigantic virus. Humans multiplied many times over, destroying the entire earth.

Freddieo Rosemont thought that by massive killings of humans, the gigantic virus would vanish, saving Mother Earth. Having massive graveyards covering as much of the earth as possible would help nourishing the earth with dead human beings full of minerals to replenish the earth's soil, recycling humans like aluminum cans, growing trees taller and turning grass greener.

F. Rosemont's kingdom killers nicknamed Freddieo the "T.V.-Boot-Loot Faggot," because of his aggressive verbal harassment, and use of his stress psychology to victimize each human he stalked for the kill. F. Rosemont's mouth ran like a machine gun, each word a bullet to stress the victim into over-reacting and not being their normal self, to accomplish the ultimate, death, maybe by car accident, speeding on the highway after work because of a raging temper, stressed out by one of F. Rosemont's kingdom killers, like a supervisor saying word for word exactly what F. Rosemont radared to their eardrums.

Or by an overdose of drugs; or a stroke, sometimes called sudden death; or self-inflicted suicide, due to seeing it was the only way to forgive oneself after going berserk, and shooting up an entire work floor or the family. F. Rosemont was a master of getting humans buried for what seemed to be no reason at all. Senseless homicides, escalating suicides at an all-time high, people going berserk and killing innocent people—only God knew for sure how many humans in one split-second instance die. Gang warfare plagued the nation, over who owned what part of a certain side of town to sell dope in and F. Rosemont was telling a gang member which postal employee had the best insurance policy for a sure hit to help the gang's dope traffic.

Darrick was not aware of the television network system viewing his every move, nor was he aware of the postal inspectors at his job also being kingdom killers, watching him like a cockroach about to be sprayed with Raid upon Linda's twin sister's, Sally's, command. Sally was nicknamed, "the Dick Stalker" because she always ate her victim's penis. Sally was also like her Uncle F. Rosemont, who knew stress kills and used it to his advantage. Sally knew how mood swings worked to her advantage, getting her victim in the right mood to have sex, then sign a pre-burial contract, or in the right mood or frame of mind to have the victim do as she wished. Her uncle's stress psychology and her mood swinging usually would cause a person to go berserk. Sally and Linda both worked at the post office and both were inspectors, inspecting who they thought was ready for their uncle's funeral parlor, but Linda had a change of heart when she fell in love with Darrick. She warned him of the dangerous funeral parlor Mafia and their kingdom killers, and practically their entire operation.

The next day at work, Darrick started telling people what Linda had told him. Sally, viewing all of Darrick's conversations and movements throughout the work floor, was wondering how in the hell Darrick had gotten hold of their Mafia's "code of silence" set of laws. Darrick was hysterically trying to convince everyone who had signed the pre-burial contract with Rosemont's Funeral Parlor to drop it immediately, because their lives were in danger. None of his co-workers believed Darrick was telling the truth. They believed he had had a bad experience over at Linda's relatives' house on Thanksgiving, and probably was not able to make out with Linda. They thought he was just trying to get even with Linda for a dead date, trying to shame her and her relatives' names, for the Rosemonts were very well liked, respected, and looked up to for leadership, and people trusted the Rosemonts to the limit.

Darrick saw that it was useless and all his efforts were a waste of time. He thought he'd give it one more try, and he started screaming on the work floor and yelling out, "The Rosemonts are out to get you, they're going to bury each and every one of you like a bunch of cockroaches, at their own will, at the time of their own choosing, for their own personal needs, whether it be money to pay for taxes, mortgage notes, a new automobile or their own satisfaction, such as having sex with a dead stiff dick or playing hole-in-one golf until the burial ceremonies with a wide-legged, dead whore on the funeral parlor carpet. Or how about stealing a corpse's reusable organs, preferably their kidneys, liver, hair, or ass buns for plastic surgery on one of the Rosemont's faces, or even taking their eyeballs and using them for household decorations, such as setting them inside a stuffed reindeer's eyes sockets—yes, a blue-eyed reindeer, with the eyeballs of a dead white person."

Everybody on the work floor started laughing at Darrick, saying, "Boy, Linda sure must have blew his mind."

Sally noticed Darrick's yelling and the disturbance he was causing on the work floor, having everybody laugh and discontinue their job performances. This nuisance had to cease and be removed from the work floor. Sally called the post office security telephone for Darrick to be removed from the work place because he was disturbing the other workers, and he seemed very disturbed about something, disoriented, confused, and giving the impression of someone about to go berserk, about to do some harm to one of his fellow co-workers if touched in the wrong way.

Sally told the post office security to take special caution, saying, "Darrick could be highly dangerous to himself and others. Shoot the son-of-a-bitch if necessary, especially if he gets violent." Post office security approached Darrick slowly and very cautiously, as if he might explode and become a vicious psychopath, stopping at nothing but a bullet if he attacked the two post office security guards.

Darrick took a deep breath as he noticed the two post office security guards, as if to say, "What the hell is the matter?" but did not say anything.

Suddenly, Darrick burst out in a loud voice, saying, "Are you the kingdom killers sent by F. Rosemont to kill me?"

One of the post office security guards shouted, "Freeze, you crazy son-of-a-bitch, before I blow your ass to kingdom come!"

Darrick, frightened to death and being asthmatic, fainted when one of the post office security guards pulled out the 357-magnum hand gun. He woke up in the Los Angeles County Hospital, on the psychiatric locked ward, strapped to a bed by police handcuffs, and had been given lithium, a powerful tranquilizer they used on elephants. Darrick had no control over his entire body. He couldn't lift his arms, legs or even open his mouth. The tranquilizers put his complete frame of mind in the Magic Kingdom, like Alice in Wonderland, about to see the Wizard of Oz. The odds were stacked against Darrick almost one hundred to zero of him convincing anybody of Linda's telephone conversation. Besides, this could have been just a crank joke by Linda to make him look like a damned arrogant, horny fool.

The psychiatrist stated that he was under mild stress syndrome from being overworked and underpaid. Working six days a week and holidays, too, plus the three hours driving every day, was just starting to show its side effects. The psychiatrist recommended a couple of weeks away from the job plus relaxation and enjoying some entertainment, maybe with his girlfriend, Linda. The psychiatrist also wrote Darrick a prescription for a mild sedative to calm his nerves, advising him to get plenty of rest. He also offered Darrick a stress therapy class lasting almost six months, to help him relieve some of the stress in his life by making him aware of what was causing his stress, and how to deal with his stress without losing control of himself, or without having an asthmatic attack, a heart attack or even cause the death of himself and others by going berserk.

Darrick came to his senses and decided to go along with the psychiatrist's suggestion, attending classes at the hospital once a week at the Los Angeles County Hospital, in the evening right after work. He preferred Mondays, the start of his work week. Darrick never realized that stress could cause all these ailments, and wanted to find out how it caused him to have an asthmatic attack and go berserk on the job. He tried to find out if it really was the miserable, dull, dusty, dungeon-like, depressing-looking work place, with some of his co-workers wearing the same clothes every day, blowing mucus out of their noses, coughing up a storm from being infected by viruses from the damned dust hanging every goddamned where like ice crystals from the ceiling, or was it the damned supervisor asking his co-workers, "How's it going?" or "How are they treating you?" every damned day.

Darrick tried to figure out what made him go berserk when he started screaming and yelling, not knowing of course it was the every two damned weeks funeral notices posted on the bulletin board. Darrick didn't know that the Rosemonts indirectly promoted hate, racism, jealousy, and ignorance, by use of the communications network, using their rented television viewing booth or by radio media.

So what if Los Angeles had one of the biggest riots in United States history, plus the largest United States fire storms caused by, they say, a careless homeless person trying to keep warm in the cold months of the year. This psychiatrist started to bring to light the key elements that the Rosemonts prospered from: besides their brainwashing, using stress psychology and different mood swings as the icing on the cake, the main ingredients to the formula of death were hate, racism, jealousy and, of course, but not the least, ignorance.

As far as racism went, why in hell would a human being think they are better than another because of his skin color—how sick! How in the world can a human being think like this? This sickness spread like cancer throughout Los Angeles, to cause the end result—death. Hundreds of people died, and were injured, hurt, or left mentally disturbed because maybe their business was burned down, or a loved one of theirs was killed, and their disturbed state of mental being was carried over to the fire storms that ravaged and heavily damaged Los Angeles, causing even more and more stress that would sooner or later explode into something more devastating and harmful to the human race as a whole, hopefully not the O.J. Simpson case. But to the Rosemonts it was Christmas, their peace on Earth, the love for death, blood hounds for Satan's hell, filling the graveyards like stone-loved vultures. The more death, the richer the Rosemonts got without a doubt, promoting death to the ultimate climax, the agents of human destruction, total mayhem and wild savagery.

The earthquakes in Los Angeles were just appetizers compared to the destruction of the Rodney King riot, ignited because a bunch of white policemen tried to change his black skin color by beating him severely with billy clubs. Add to that the fire storm started by, they say, a homeless person trying to keep warm. Gee whiz, he sure gets around town, doesn't he, like Jimmy the Cricket, fires starting up every damn where. After all the shit, a general feeling of keeping the peace began in Los Angeles by getting a new Los Angeles Police Department Chief, and the Rodney King verdict of not guilty given to the Los Angeles policemen who did the beating of Rodney King was reversed to guilty for using too much arresting force, violating Rodney King's civil rights and causing extreme mental and physical damage as well.

But the Rosemonts say, "Hell, no!! We don't want no damned peace in Los Angeles." The Rosemonts pushed their perfect opportunity of damned near ruling the entire city of Los Angeles to the max. They wanted to get rid of people who thought for themselves, who weren't programmed to the television and radio media like robots, doing and buying products as they saw and heard on television or radio; and most of all, who weren't doing what they demanded on the post office work floor, as they used them for the Rosemonts' personal needs, killing them like cockroaches at will.

Now, achieving another personal satisfaction of F. Rosemont was eating away at his guts—killing D. Price Jones at any cost, whatever it took to rid his system of this nuisance son-of-a-bitch trying to warn people of his funeral parlor Mafia. But the thing tearing away at his heart was this commoner, Darrick, having his favorite niece, Linda, fall in love with this common cockroach. This disturbed Freddieo so much that he had overloaded Darrick's Thanksgiving dinner with tranquilizers to cause a massive stroke right before his and Linda's eyes. He was frankly disappointed that the lucky son-of-a-bitch, cockroach, crawling bastard was saved by Linda, which just added to the must die, motherfucker desire Freddieo had for Darrick.

The price of death Freddieo Rosemont put on Darrick's head was priceless—at any and all cost, this son-of-a-bitch must die and be buried in his graveyard, in a place especially reserved for Darrick, a hole not six feet deep, but twelve feet deep, already dug out under a sesame seed tree full of nests for bats and vultures that constantly dropped their bird shit in Darrick's reserved grave burial hole. Freddieo hoped it would be half-full of bird shit by the time Darrick was killed by the kingdom killers.

Freddieo summoned the kingdom killers to kill him any way and sooner than later, with the reward being the largest they had ever seen—a new mansion fully paid for by Freddieo himself was the prize rewarded for the dead body of Darrick Price Jones. With a reward like that, Darrick was sooner than later to be dead.

Darrick arrived at work earlier than usual the next work day, somewhat less stressed out because his psychiatrist had him on a mild sedative, keeping him calm and his nerves at ease, when Linda came running, grabbing him around his waist, holding him tightly, as if for the first and final time, saying, "Dear Lord, you're alive! I thought maybe they took you away to be killed when someone told me they took you away in handcuffs on a push hand truck they use for pushing around mail, security guards pushing you on the elevator like you were a sack of mail. But they say you passed out or had another asthmatic attack."

Darrick told Linda he was taken to the hospital's psychiatric locked ward and given a strong tranquilizer that made him immobile, and a psychiatrist told him he had mild stress and suggested he has stress therapy class once a week at the Los Angeles County Hospital. It was held each Monday after his job, in the evenings, to help handle his stress without going berserk or doing something that he would regret later.

Linda expressed her satisfaction at seeing Darrick alive and well, and spent a little time on the elevator exchanging intimate kisses. This was a safe place, Linda thought, knowing about the closed circuit television monitoring system, but she was wrong. The elevator had secret hidden viewing electronic devices especially for catching employees in such an act as their kissing or having sexual intercourse or even smoking dope or drinking alcohol and fighting.

Sally, Linda's twin sister, observed all their explicit activity from her viewing booth and called her Uncle Freddieo Rosemont. Freddieo was so furiously angry, mad and frustrated about this forbidden occurrence, that he called his kingdom killers to kill Darrick immediately, making the reward more handsome than ever before by adding a gold Rolls Royce of his along with the new mansion.

With an offer like that, Darrick was for sure a sitting duck ready to be roasted, not realizing how hungry Freddieo had made his kingdom killers to have Darrick Price Jones arrive in kingdom come, dead, six feet under, on top of six feet of some batty vultures' bird shit. Freddieo decided to bury this nuisance, this nerve-wrecking, revolutionary, piece of shit Darrick, scot free, all expenses paid for, in his exclusive graveyard high in the Belair Mountains. Freddieo even threw in some tulip flowers filled with his own shit to be placed on top of Darrick's grave after he was buried in six feet of bird shit and six feet of dirt.

Linda told Darrick what her uncle was going to do to them if they were seen together, especially romancing. She told him how her uncle disapproved of a commoner like Darrick getting close to her and that their relationship was forbidden, and would pay death to Darrick if he was ever caught or seen with her. She stated that their forbidden love had to be kept secret and told him that he never should have started telling people about her uncle's funeral parlor Mafia and the kingdom killers. He was lucky to be alive because the post office security guards were some of her uncle's kingdom killers, and that if he hadn't fainted from his asthmatic attack, he probably would have been shot to death by the post office security.

Darrick wanted to believe Linda but was having a hard time, not really sure if she was or wasn't telling the truth, if she was playing with his mind, trying to make a complete ass of him, or if she really was telling the truth and really loved him. He had no sound material evidence, but he did know one thing for sure, he was hospitalized twice after just a short time dating Linda.

Maybe Linda was too much for him to handle, maybe too much sex, and being overworked and the three hours a day driving was starting to cause side effects in him, like shouting at work and fainting asthmatic attacks all of a sudden. Darrick and Linda kissed each other good-bye on the elevator and each went their separate way to their respective work assignment. Darrick was a clerk and Linda was in the management field of the post office, accounting for mail volume and total man hours needed for each eight hour swing shift, plus inspecting post office employees.

Darrick went and sat on his stool to separate the mail according to zip code, with a cloud of dust hanging over his head, looking like an ice crystal on the ceiling. Linda and Sally both shared the same television viewing booth when smoke slowly started filling the work area Darrick was sitting in. Someone finally shouted, "Fire, fire, fire!" and the fire alarm sounded, loudly—but not so loudly that when Darrick thought he heard gunshots, he was right.

Linda shouted to Darrick to hit the floor and lay flat. One of his fellow workers, the one who wore the same clothes every day, had a 357-magnum hand gun, and was shooting, shooting, shooting and then reloading, hitting and wounding and killing only the Lord knows how many of Darrick's co-workers, until one of the security guards for the post office finally landed a bullet directly into his head, killing him instantly. Ambulances, fire trucks, paramedics, television crews, and Los Angeles Police Department investigators were everywhere, trying to count the dead, wounded and hurt.

Finally they put out the fire, the smoke cleared a little and Darrick had the picture of an awful scene he had never imagined before in his life, that he would actually see about two dozen dead bodies, fellow co-workers, dead right before his very eyes. A tear rolled slowly down his cheekbone, as he looked at the paramedics carrying away the wounded and hurt, some yelling and screaming, saying, "God, please save me!" Some cursing, saying, "Goddamn it, that crazy son-of-a-bitch."

Finally all the smoke cleared and blood was all over the work floor and mail was scattered everywhere, with the stools and mail cases trampled, caused by this common, everyday, plain, happy-go-lucky, nice, quiet guy who went berserk and on a killing rampage. Darrick thought the was dreaming, having a nightmare. How in heaven's name could a nice guy like that start shooting so many people dead? He always attended his fellow co-workers' funerals and donated money to help a fellow co-worker in need, and had been one of the nicest people one would ever want to run across. He never bothered anyone, and mostly kept to himself, a Catholic church-going individual who went to church every Sunday. He was never selfish and always gave his last dollar to help any co-worker in need. He didn't even seem like the type of person to own a gun, and acted like he wouldn't hurt a fly. A generous, considerate, thoughtful, caring individual, all of a sudden looking like he was possessed, out of a twilight zone, in a deep trance, controlled by the unknown, pulling the trigger on that hand gun that killed twenty-four people upon impact of the 357 bullet. What could have possibly caused him to do such a thing?

First there was the smoke, then the shooting. Linda came out of the television viewing booth, yelling out Darrick's name and running toward him, grabbing him around his waist, shaking, as nervous as someone standing in front of a firing squad about to be shot to death for murder. She was crying, frightened to death of possibly being yet another victim of the awful, bloody human slaughter. Darrick comforted her, rocking her back and forth as they were standing, assuring her there was no more danger present. He looked at his friend whom had gone berserk all of a sudden being carried away by homicide detectives, his body covered with white sheets showing some blood stains from the bullet embedded in his head that killed him instantly, knocking him to the floor like a knock-down punch thrown by a prize fighter. Some of the detectives and CBS News reporters were inquiring why in heaven's name would a simple, everyday, ordinary postal clerk go berserk like that.

The CBS reporter finally came over to Darrick and Linda, excusing himself from interrupting their private moment of despair. He spoke to them both at the same time, saying, "Excuse me for one moment, please. Sorry to disturb you at a moment like this, but I'm a news reporter for the 10:00 P.M. news on the CBS network station. I am inquiring as to the possibility of the insane shooting that just took place. From the majority of postal workers whom I have interviewed, they have stated that this was probably brought on from verbal harassment from his supervisor and a removal notice he stated he received in his mail yesterday from his supervisor, pending further investigation as to if he was eating or chewing Doublemint chewing gum he bought from the candy machine.

"The other workers stated they had had a big argument over that incident two days before this all happened. His supervisor stated he was eating his lunch while he was checking the mail by zip codes. One of his co-workers stated that his supervisor started calling him an outright liar and this was really when he became very tense and nervous. He started shaking as if he was about to lose his self-control, standing face-to-face, almost toe-to-toe, the two were. Arguing back and forth over something as simple as chewing gum or eating a banana from his lunch bag which the supervisor accused him of.

"The gunman's temper started getting intense and his voice was getting louder also. Their shouting at one another started interrupting the other workers. The gunman, named Ralph, started accusing his supervisor, named Mr. Smith, of always harassing him, just to be doing something, pushing his authority around to help his ego and image to make Ralph feel like a damn dog, since he already had to look for aluminum pop cans inside of post office trash cans on his lunch hour, to afford the high cost of living and make ends meet in Los Angeles, California.

"So, anyway, the next day, the head boss of the post office building, Mr. Ross, followed up on the accusation of whether or not he was eating his lunch or chewing a stick of Doublemint chewing gum. Everybody for some strange reason stated that he probably was eating his lunch, but were not quite sure. No one actually saw him take a bite of his lunch, the banana.

"The next day when Ralph came to work, he stated he received a letter for his removal. He was being fired pending an investigation by the boss himself, Mr. Ross. Another one of your co-workers stated that this morning, Ralph seemed entirely disturbed and angry about something. Finally," the reporter stated, "someone saw Ralph in the rest room, shaking, standing in front of the mirror. He appeared as though he was making faces, looking strange and mad about something."

The reporter, almost out of breath, asked if Darrick or Linda had anything to say or add to his nightly news report, to be aired at 10:00 P.M. on the CBS network that night, saying their comments would be highly appreciated and rewarding if they had any clues at all as to why this tragic incident happened.

Darrick, still somewhat shocked, stated that he was a very nice, quiet, innocent type of individual. He was very surprised to see this happen, especially from someone who wouldn't hurt a mouse.

Linda, getting her nerves in order, said, "My uncle, F. Rosemont, says that the stress level at the post office is very high and something like this was bound to happen. He's in the funeral business."

The reported stated, "Oh, yes, Mr. Rosemont. I know him. He's a very respectable man. I run into him from time to time at the CBS TV studio network building." Neither one of them knew that Freddieo was viewing this from the closed circuit cable television, and heard every word and was very pleased at the outcome. This was good for his funeral parlor business—twenty-four dead bodies, and all the cockroaches had signed the pre-burial contract to be buried by his funeral parlor. But he was still highly in a state of rage, staring at the unpleasant living sight of that fucking cockroach, that motherfucker, Darrick.

The reporter thanked them both for their comments and enlightenment on the tragic incident, and told them both to take care and peace be with them. But peace was out of the question as Darrick took Linda to her apartment, located in the Wilshire area of Los Angeles, called "The Miracle Mile," just a few minutes from the post office but directly in the eyesight and killing distance of her murderous and notorious Uncle Freddieo, who was staring his hateful eyeballs out, waiting for Darrick to leave his niece and head for his house in his GT Mustang five-speed stick shift.

Finally, Darrick kissed Linda good-bye, assuring her once again that everything was going to be all right and not to worry the least bit. Leaving Linda in a peaceful state of mind, he turned the key to start the motor of his high-performance automobile. He only had about a one-and-a-half hour drive home to Riverside, California, where he had bought a two-bedroom house about ten years ago at a reasonable price, before the real estate market in his neighborhood skyrocketed, making his house unaffordable if he were to purchase it at today's highway robbery prices.

There were about only thirty minutes left before he would pick up his telephone and hear from his love, Linda. Listening to the local radio station and one of his favorite tunes, called "I'll Be There," he thought he was still at work when he heard yet more gunshots. He thought he was having flashbacks, memories of the tragic death-filled nightmare at work. But he wasn't having flashbacks at all; there was a man shooting bullets at his car approximately one hundred yards behind his GT Mustang.

One bullet struck his car trunk, another striking the rear glass and going through the front glass of his passenger side. Darrick panicked—all this violence was too much for him to handle. He threw his car into fifth gear and sped out from the flow of traffic, almost losing control of his car as he barely missed several other cars on the Interstate 10 eastbound highway during the rush hour traffic.

He was wondering who this son-of-a-bitch could or might be that was chasing him, shooting bullets at his car as he was coasting ninety miles an hour, barely dodging cars, toward his home, where he had his only weapon, a 45-caliber hand gun. At this high speed and with the gunman on his tail shooting a couple of more bullets at his car but missing it, Darrick made a hard, fast right and another hard, fast left, the bullets striking an innocent driver in the back of his head, causing his car to go completely out of control, almost spinning around in the opposite direction of the flow of traffic, before the driver's car was struck by several cars, sending his car tumbling over and over, causing a massive car pile-up, and the gunman somewhere in the middle of all the mess.

There were about a hundred or more cars and vehicles piled up, Darrick noticed as he looked in his rear view mirror and made his exit off the highway to his home on Riverside Boulevard in the city of Riverside. Freddieo, watching the driving adventure with tense emotions, said to himself this must be his lucky day, the highway fatalities caused by the driver of the car the bullet unfortunately struck in the back of his head, was estimated at thirty dead as reported by Sky Watch, a radio station helicopter, reporting highway traffic jams, accidents and fatalities on Radio Dial 101 FM.

Freddieo was more than pleased at the outcome—maybe some of the dead's relatives might want his funeral parlor to bury some of the highway fatalities. Although he was pleased that it was a good day for business, he was angry as all hell that Darrick didn't get killed by one of his kingdom killers he summoned out to take care of the unpleasant face that was always showing up alive, unhurt and untouched. That goddamned Darrick Price Jones must die before the sun came up in the morning, in about twelve more hours, it being about seven PM. Darrick opened his door and called Linda immediately. Linda answered the phone on the second ring.

Darrick, highly emotional, stressed out from all the unexpected activities of today, exclaimed, "Linda, you would never believe what just happened on the highway as I was driving home, about fifteen minutes ago!"

But before Darrick could finish saying what he had to say, Linda shouted, "Darrick, you had better watch out. My uncle, he just called me, saying he was going to kill your ass before the sun rises in the morning! He told me he would and I guess he meant it! That was one of his kingdom killers he sent out to kill you. Lucky for you, the other driver caught the bullet that was meant for you!"

Darrick now believed every word Linda had told him on the phone the other day when she first mentioned the funeral parlor Mafia run by her Uncle Freddieo and his kingdom killers. Now he believed Linda really loved him, believing that if it wasn't for her, he would have been dead for sure at her uncle's Thanksgiving dinner table when he had the asthmatic attack, caused from her uncle loading his turkey dressing with tranquilizers, or the berserk post office rampage killing spree that was caused by her uncle using stress psychology on the fellow, Ralph, who dressed the same every day, by telling his supervisor to harass him for chewing gum.

One of the 357-magnum bullets could easily have killed him if he were at his work site, where all the others were shot, instead of in the elevator, romancing Linda. Darrick figured Linda saved his life twice and he owed it to her to save her life from being controlled by her ruthless, notorious, grave-digging, murderous, mad uncle. Linda all of a sudden told Darrick she had to go because it was her Uncle Freddieo banging at her door. She hung up the telephone before Darrick could say how much he really loved her and how he should never had doubted her word for one minute.

It was Linda's uncle at the door and he ordered Linda to get her belongings together right away and come live with him, having a violent behavior Linda had never seen before in her life.

Shouting at her, angry as all hell, raging with a temper that was about to explode into yet another mad man about to go berserk, he said to Linda, almost shouting at her, "Do you know that son-of-a-bitch, cockroach, motherfucker, common shithead caused one of my kingdom killers to be killed in a car wreck while chasing his asshole down the highway, shooting bullets at his goddamn car?"

"No, my dearest uncle," replied Linda in a soft but frightened voice.

"So I had another one of my killers set a time bomb in his house that is about to go off, in about thirty minutes from now, my sweetest niece, so you can certainly get that damn commoner out of your pretty little brain."

Linda started screaming, "No! No! No!!!" and reaching for the telephone to warn Darrick of the time bomb, but Freddieo grabbed her by the waist, picking her up off the floor and handing her over to one of his kingdom killers, to be taken to his gold Rolls Royce.

Meanwhile, Darrick, back at the house, decided to load his 45 semi-automatic hand gun and go after Freddieo, while the time bomb was ticking away, leaving only about five minutes before Darrick would be blown to kingdom come by the time bomb set there by yet another one of Freddieo's kingdom killers. He was as mad as all hell from the brief conversation with Linda. He immediately jumped in his GT once again, not to be chased by a gunman sent by Freddieo, but to be a gunman for Freddieo. Turning the key to his car, the engine roaring like a hail storm, he floored the gas pedal to the floor, pounding off car tire rubber like he had never done before in his life, sounding like a 747 jet plane about to take off from a landing strip.

Looking in his rear view mirror at the corner on his block, he saw and heard his house explode into shattering pieces of wood, off its foundation of concrete as the time bomb exploded, just as he was at the corner about to enter onto the highway, a safe distance from the tremendous explosion. He said out loud to himself, "Well, I'll be goddamned, I could have been dead!"

Now Darrick was as much after Freddieo as Freddieo was after him, or even more so, seeing how his house was blown to pieces by one of Freddieo's kingdom killers. This was it, either him or me, contemplated Darrick, doing ninety-five miles an hour this time to Freddieo's mansion in Belair, California, on Interstate 10 westbound to Los Angeles, dodging cars and slamming on the brakes to keep from having rear-end collisions. He figured if he could dodge flying speeding bullets, he could dodge all the traffic on the highway to Freddieo's mansion.

First, he decided to stop by Linda's apartment to see if she was there, but by the time he arrived at her apartment, the door was left wide open. Darrick ran in with his gun cocked in his hand, shouting, "Linda, Linda! Linda, where are you, sweetheart?"

Seeing no trace of Linda and the phone off the hook, Darrick knew something terrible must have happened to her. Hoping it wasn't too late to save her from her insane Uncle Freddieo, he jumped back into his car, floored the gas pedal once again, peeling rubber from his car tires, and roared down the streets to Freddieo's mansion at the top of Belair Mountain, on the edge of a steep cliff overlooking the deep valley about two miles below, where there was nothing but vast, empty desert, and on the opposite side, overlooking the city of Lost Angels.

About one-half mile from the mansion, parallel to and on the same level grounds of Freddieo's mansion, was the massive graveyard Freddieo owned and where he had already dug that grave for Darrick, half-filled with bat and vulture bird shit. Freddieo's graveyard covered two square miles of the Belair mountain top, looking like a ghostly enchanted rain forest surrounded by ten feet of marble stone used as a fence for his dead bodies. Freddieo knew for sure that Darrick was somewhere in another world, perhaps the twilight zone, blown to kingdom come by one of his kingdom killers that put a time bomb on his roof when Darrick was talking to Linda on the telephone about the highway incident. But how surprised Freddieo would be to see a dead person come alive and spook the living hell out of him.

As he was coming closer to Freddieo's heavenly landscaped mansion on top of Belair Mountain, the sun was going down beyond the horizon, turning day into night, and the moon, full in its entirety, glowed, lighting the earth with its full-moon brilliance, lighting for Darrick the path to the psychopath Freddieo, ruler of the funeral parlor Mafia, who thought he could save Mother Earth from being destroyed from being overpopulated with humans.

Darrick finally neared the top of Belair Mountain, seeing the sight of Freddieo's mansion and the towering water fountain tossing water high above the Freddieo Mansion, almost hiding it completely, looking like a sparkling waterfall.

He knew he was near the right mansion grounds as he came closer to the towering water fountain in the front yard of Freddieo's mansion. Closing in, slowly, driving without his headlights on at about five miles per hour, he saw Freddieo's gold Rolls Royce parked in front of the huge double door entrance of the three-level white marble mansion.

Darrick, approximately two hundred yards from the mansion, decided to park his car and creep around to the back door, hoping to climb through one of the windows and sneak around inside until coming upon Freddieo, then shooting him dead. But it so happened that Freddieo was having a meeting with all of his kingdom killers, celebrating the deaths of the postal clerks and, of course, that goddamn nuisance, Darrick, and rewarding the mansion and gold Rolls Royce to the kingdom killer who planted the time bomb on Darrick's roof. They were positively sure Darrick was still indoors when the bomb exploded, blowing him up and his house off of its foundation. How could anyone possibly live? But lucky for Darrick, aggravated by Linda's telephone call, he had left about fifteen seconds before the bomb rocked the entire neighborhood, and viewed the explosion from his rear view mirror as he was about to enter onto the highway.

Entering into Freddieo's mansion through the glass sliding door in the back yard that he opened with a piece of clothing wire, he slipped through the metal that was enclosing the glass window, unhooking the lock with a hard twist of his hand. Locking the glass window again once inside the mansion, Darrick, with his forty-five hand gun in his right hand, cocked and ready to shoot, snuck down the hallway to their kingdom killer meeting place, where he heard laughter and loud voices bragging about how they knocked off the post office clerks like cockroaches, while drinking their alcohol and rewarding the one kingdom killer named Dick Angelo who finally blew Darrick to kingdom come.

No one was paying attention to anything else, because this was a celebration of all times—a total of twenty-five dead post office clerks all in one day, just by Freddieo having a post office stressed out. By telling his supervisor to say word for word what he said by using his advanced radar sound technology in the closed circuit cable television studio booth, radaring Freddieo's voice so only the supervisor could hear what Freddieo said, to stress the everyday, common, pop can trash-picker named Ralph into going berserk, and finally shooting up the post office clerks, all twenty-three, and finally being shot to death by the security guard, making a total of twenty-four dead, two dozen cockroaches.

All the dead cockroaches had pre-burial Rosemont's Funeral Parlor contracts. Why, to Freddieo, it was almost like winning a jackpot state lottery. All the post office clerks had big life insurance policies; for sure their loved ones would ask for the elaborate, expensive burial plan with all the burial extras—gold and silver trimmed caskets, with a full orchestra or renting their favorite singer, Aretha Franklin, maybe, singing through the entire burial ceremony. Why adding up each individual post office employee's burial cost, he would for sure come out a lot wealthier and, of course, burying Darrick Price Jones for free, if the police department could find all or any of his body parts.

Linda was tranquilized and put into a deep sleep while all of this celebration was going on. Darrick automatically figured that Freddieo was there, entertaining his kingdom killers. As he crept slowly through the hallway where he first kissed Linda, toward the huge door where he heard the loud voices and laughter, Darrick had his gun cocked, ready to start shooting his fourteen-bullet clip from his semi-automatic 45-caliber hand gun. He was about to open the huge door, grabbing the door handle, when suddenly someone grabbed Darrick's hand from the door handle. Darrick, shocked, panicked, and turned quickly, about to pull the trigger on his cocked gun, but was outrageously astounded to see his love, Linda, or so he thought.

"Linda, Linda," in a soft, whispering voice Darrick said. "You're all right!"

"Yes, my darling love, I'm all right!" Surprisingly, she answered, kissing him into a profound idiot, then suddenly spraying him with black pepper spray, knocking him unconscious instantly, for it was not Linda at all, but her twin sister, Fast Sally.

Sally turned the handle on the huge door, opening it and finally shouted out to her Uncle Freddieo, "Freddieo! Freddieo! Freddieo! It's that nuisance, cockroach, son-of-a-bitch Darrick once again!"

"Why, goddamn it, that motherfucker, cockroach, son-of-a-bitch—how in the hell does that bastard stay alive?" shouted Freddieo, stressed out more than ever before, just like he stress killed the post office employees by stressing out the common, everyday, same-dressed, post office clerk, Ralph, by telling his supervisor to falsely accuse Ralph of eating a banana.

Now, Darrick was stressing Freddieo out by being alive, failed murder attempt after murder attempt, just seeing this common shithead punk pop up at his celebration of the dead post office clerks was almost enough to make him go berserk himself.

Freddieo ran over, screaming, "Goddamn it!" to see it was really the same damned Darrick Price Jones. He looked Darrick square in the face as Darrick was lying unconscious on the red wool carpet. Freddieo snatched Darrick's hand gun out of his hand and cocked the 45 semi-automatic to shoot the bastard son-of-a-bitch in the face who was making his life so miserable.

Freddieo started calling out loud, "You living-dead nuisance cockroach!" He caught hold of himself and said, "I don't want this damn cockroach's blood all over my beautiful red wool carpet." Uncocking the trigger on the 45 semi-automatic he had against Darrick's unconscious skull with a look of despair and hatred, he took control of his face. Freddieo started kicking Darrick furiously as he was lying still and unconscious yet, trying to bring him back to consciousness, kicking him harder and harder, like he was a piece of shit or a soccer ball, until Darrick finally regained consciousness, shaking his head and saying, "What happened, where am I?"

Freddieo shouted at him like he had become a damned psychopath all of a sudden, saying, "You say something else, you smart son-of-a-bitch, I'll blow your fucking brains out of your fucking skull!!!"

Sally, becoming very emotional, kicked Darrick in his face, saying, "That's what you get for my kisses, you common piece of shit!!!" She almost knocked the heel of her high heel shoe off when she struck Darrick across his mouth with her right foot, leaving Darrick with a busted upper lip.

Freddieo, about to lose his self-control from seeing the unexpected sight of a motherfucker who was supposed to be dead, shouted out his anger and stress with the raising of his voice, saying to the rest of his kingdom killers, "Tie the son-of-a-bitch up and put a paper grocery bag over his goddamned bird shit face. I'm going to make damned sure I kill this cockroach."

Darrick was tied with rope, with his hands in his back and his ankles together, and thrown in the back trunk of Freddieo's gold Rolls Royce by a dozen of his kingdom killers, all dressed in black suits. Tape was placed across Darrick's mouth before they slammed the trunk shut so he was not able to make a sound or yell for help. Freddieo was getting ready to make sure Darrick didn't escape his love for death because he was going to take him to his graveyard and cover his dead body with a marble stone, about three feet wide and tall, with Darrick Price Jones' name already carved in the marble stone, saying "Stone Love" under Darrick's name, because Freddieo was especially in love with Darrick paying with his life for his burial ground and his funeral expenses, all free of charge.

He was anxiously awaiting the moment to finally see this nuisance, cockroach, motherfucker, son-of-a-bitch, bastard buried, just for wasting so much of his time trying to get him killed. And making love to his niece, Linda, had taken his nerves to the limit. He was about to go berserk himself if he didn't see that Darrick was covered with his prime dirt, enriched by the other dead bodies laying in his massive graveyard where there was peace and solitude. Definitely this was where Freddieo would get his peace of mind, from his rain forest graveyard grounds with thousands of dead bodies, the most beautiful forestry in the city of Los Angeles, California.

Here at Freddieo's graveyard grounds, he thought the dead were fertilizing, replenishing and renourishing Mother Earth, instead of living human beings destroying the earth. Freddieo believed he was the savior of Mother Earth, feeding the earth with dead bodies, like a living organism. Freddieo thought he was a god, seeing as he saw fit; in his point of view, all humans were cockroaches. He was causing death amongst humans who he thought would fertilize Mother Earth the best, instead of the damned human beings destroying Mother Earth's resources and minerals, polluting the air, and destroying the ozone layer, which would definitely cause Mother Earth's death.

So, there was Darrick in the back of Freddieo's car trunk, ready to be eaten by Mother Earth after he was put to death by Freddieo personally, who would make sure the cockroach, son-of-a-bitch didn't escape or survive any mishaps or misfortunes on the part of one of Freddieo's kingdom killers. Freddieo was personally going to put a 45-caliber bullet square in the middle of Darrick's skull, with his own semi-automatic, 45-caliber hand gun, having Darrick stand directly in front of the batty, vulture bird shit half-filled grave all ready and waiting especially for the damn nuisance, Darrick Price Jones.

Finally, at last, the price for Darrick was right—free, buried free, on the house, at no cost, and with a marble stone carved in gold letters, saying, "Darrick Price Jones, 'Stone Love', I love you to death, from Freddieo Rosemont." So, jumping in his gold Rolls Royce with Darrick in his trunk all neatly tied and "good to go," Freddieo drove to his lush, elaborate, rain-forest, peace-of-mind graveyard, where thousands of dead bodies were feeding Mother Earth, making the grass turn greener, almost blue-green, and the trees grow taller and fuller. Freddieo led the way, with all his kingdom killers trailing, to Darrick Price Jones' grave site. About a hundred kingdom killers were waiting to see the end of this troublesome son-of-a-bitch, to be killed by their boss.

Back at Freddieo's mansion, Fast Sally went and woke up Linda. She told her that the damn-fool cockroach, Darrick, had tried to kill Freddieo, and she had caught him as he was about to open the door to their meeting quarters while they were celebrating the death of all the post office clerks.

"When I grabbed his hand, he turned, looking me dead in my face and started saying the strangest things. I almost burst out laughing, but I kept my composure. He said, 'Linda, Linda, thank God you're all right,' and then the damn fool kissed me on my mouth and I pulled out my 'knock them out spray,' black pepper, and sprayed the damn fool in his face, knocking him out cold. That was when I opened the door and called Freddieo out loud. Baby, you should have seen how mad he got. He almost blew Darrick's fucking brains out on the red wool carpet, but Freddieo had a change of heart.

"I guess he decided to blow his fucking brains out in front of the grave he already prepared for him, half-filled with bat and vulture bird shit that drops from the sesame seed tree they always nest in, dug directly under their nest so birds could fill it up with their bird shit. So Darrick, the common, shitty son-of-a-bitch, would drop dead in the middle of the shit, for shitting around with you, Linda. Freddieo told me to take you to see Darrick for the last time. He said he's going to shoot him in his fucking head, with his own hand gun, so that he would fall dead on his face in his grave full of bat and vulture bird shit."

Fast Sally started laughing out loud, almost crying from her laughter, finally saying, "Now, Linda, let's go to the graveyard and see this nuisance, cockroach, motherfucker catch bird shit in his motherfucking mouth!"

Sally started laughing again, as tears rolled out of her eyes again. Linda was silent, not saying a word, because she knew Sally had a crush on her, and remembered how they used to kiss each other very often when they were younger. Linda and Sally jumped in one of the gold Rolls Royces parked in front of the mansion and were on their way to Darrick for the last time, both in extreme suspense. Linda was also a very nervous wreck and afraid that Darrick was already shot in the head and it was too late to save him. For Linda, nicknamed Proud Mary, was too proud and had too much pride and love for Darrick to let her ruthless Uncle Freddieo just kill him, her love, just to make an example for her not to mix with commoners.

Meanwhile, Darrick was driven to his grave, in the sight of a haunted night with a full moon, with the abundance of forestry looking like a rain forest. Its thickness covered the event of death about to take place, with Darrick standing in front of his grave, twelve feet deep, six feet already filled with bird shit, and with his hands tied behind his back and blindfolded, he shivered with tenseness all over his body; his knees started to shake, rattling like the sound of a rattlesnake; and his mouth was also wrapped so that he couldn't utter a single word.

Breathless, he was about to have another asthmatic attack, turning a pale color in the face, feeling faint and dizzy in the head, swaying his entire body back and forth, just about to drop into the grave hole and drown in bat and vulture bird shit, when he suddenly heard the voice he thought he would never hear again. It was Linda calling out Darrick's name as loud as she could, screaming, "Darrick! Darrick! Darrick!!!"

Freddieo and all of his kingdom killers turned around, somewhat shocked that Linda was still showing affection and love for Darrick. This made Freddieo's temper rage inside; shooting a bullet just above Darrick's head, he hit the sesame seed tree and all the bats and vulture birds flew away that were nesting there, sounding like the hounds of hell, escaping from Satan's madness, as Freddieo shouted to Linda, "That was just a warning shot, my pretty little Linda. The next bullet is going in his fucking head. This piece of cockroach-bird shit is going to be an example for you, to last you for the rest of your life. No common son-of-a-bitch makes love to my blood, and no blood of mine is going to mix blood with a piece of cockroach common shit!"

Shouting, Freddieo was as mad as all hell, about to go insane, and just the sight of this nuisance was stressing Freddieo to the point that he ordered his kingdom killers to grab Linda and stand her directly next to Darrick so that she could see him fall directly in the six feet of bird shit-filled grave hole.

Linda screamed, "Stop it!!! Stop it!!! Stop it!!!! Don't do this to Darrick. He belongs to me. You can't take him away from me!"

Linda broke loose and grabbed Darrick by the waist, embracing him like he was a part of her body. Three kingdom killers finally separated her from Darrick, holding her a few yards from him as he fell to the ground directly in front of his grave, with his face in the dirt that was to cover his dead body. He couldn't get up because he had rope tightly tied around his ankles.

Freddieo shouted, shooting Darrick's hand gun in the air, until there was only one bullet left in the clip for Darrick, saying to his kingdom killers, "Stand the goddamn son-of-a-bitch back on his feet so I can show Linda that Darrick's damn blood ain't my blood when I put this last 45-caliber bullet between his eyes, so that his goddamn contaminated blood will pour out of his forehead like a water fountain, and to show the damn piece of shit and all other shit that may come after him, that I, Freddieo Rosemont, am God, the savior of Mother Earth, head of the funeral parlor Mafia spread across the country, nationwide. I am feeding this piece of shit named Darrick Price Jones to the earth to fertilize the sesame seed tree that his motherfucking grave is dug directly under and one step in back of you, you goddamn bastard, half-full of bat and vulture bird shit!" He laughed out loud and his laughter carried over into the rest of the kingdom killers.

Everyone started laughing, except for Darrick and Linda. Laughter filled the entire graveyard, like a bunch of ghosts laughing in their graveyard, having a joke on the living, simple, innocent, common postal worker named Darrick Price Jones, who, like a fool, fell stone in love with Linda Angelo, when her relatives were a bunch of killers who killed for their funeral parlor business owned by the boss, Freddieo Rosemont, who was about to put a bullet between his eyes just for falling stone in love with his niece, who was just a few yards away, standing with three kingdom killers holding her by her arms and waist.

The laughter finally came to a halt and a complete silence came over the entire graveyard as Freddieo slowly raised the 45-caliber hand gun, and pointed it firmly and squarely between the eyes of Darrick, cocked back the hammer on the hand gun, about to squeeze the trigger and end the life of Darrick, who had fallen in love with the wrong woman, Linda Angelo, the niece of the notorious Mafia boss, Freddieo.

Freddieo was about thirty yards from Darrick, with ninety-seven kingdom killers standing at attention behind him. Linda, shaking and kicking the three kingdom killers, suddenly burst out, saying, "Fuck you, you goddamn, psychopathic, killing, son-of-a-bitch Freddieo, if you shoot the one I love, I'll kill you, and I swear to it, as I stand right before you with your one hundred kingdom killers standing in your graveyard!"

Linda's pride and love for Darrick wouldn't allow such a thing to happen to him. Freddieo snapped back his head, angry and showing signs of being stressed, shouting, "Why, you goddamn bitch, don't you ever threaten me again or I will disown your ass and put you in that damn bird shit grave hole with the piece of shit, Darrick, you're cursing me out over!"

Linda snapped yet again at her uncle, saying, "I'm not lying, goddamn it. I will kill you, if you kill the one I love!"

Freddieo turned the gun and pointed it at Linda, saying stressfully, "Goddamn you, bitch, you don't ever put a piece of shit over me, I'm your blood and you're the same blood as I am!!"

Linda shouted, "Fuck you, fuck you! Goddamn killer, I hate your fucking guts, I wish I never killed for you or suckered so many into this goddamn, hell hole graveyard for you. I wish you were dead, you damn killer!!!"

A shot rang out and Linda fell, shot, to the ground, and another shot rang out and Freddieo fell to the ground, as Sally shot Freddieo in the back for shooting Linda.

Then there were several more shots ringing out, as Sally fell, shot, falling to the ground. And Darrick finally fainted, falling to the ground, and then there was a sudden loud rumbling and the earth started to shake as all the kingdom killers pulled their hand guns, and Dick Angelo shot the kingdom killer who shot Sally Angelo.

As the earthquake was in progress, accidental shootings took place, the kingdom killers accidentally shooting each other as the 6.0 earthquake shook the ground underneath their feet, causing a complete graveyard slaughter. Each and every kingdom killer was dead and the earth stopped shaking as Darrick finally woke up from a vulture bird biting him on the neck, trying to have him for a meal. He looked around, seeing no one standing, but all lying dead in the graveyard, with blood pouring out of their bodies from bullet wounds from each others' guns, as the bats and vultures were having a feast from their dead bodies.

Darrick stood up, breaking the ropes he had tied around his ankles and hands, and spotted Linda, lying with blood pouring out of her leg. She had been wounded by her Uncle Freddieo, something he didn't mean to do, but he had got stressed out and shot Linda in the leg with the bullet meant for Darrick. Darrick went over and kissed Linda on the lips. She wasn't dead like all the rest—Freddieo, Sally, and the one hundred kingdom killers.

Linda, smiling, breathless, said, "I'm stone in love with you." Darrick carried Linda out of the graveyard, with a full moon glowing.